Blood Moon Rising
Bloodbound Covenant

Lenena Ronheer

Prologue

Murder is nothing new to Isla Crowley, hunting killers is her job. But when a body turns up drained of blood in a grim alleyway of Manchester, the crime feels *wrong*. The signs are there, too clean, too precise, and marked by an energy she knows all too well.

Vampires.

For centuries, the blood-drinkers have remained hidden, ruled by old, ironclad laws that forbid their kind from preying openly on humans. But something, or someone, has started breaking those rules. As more bodies surface, Isla, her human partner Camilla, and supernatural expert Elias find themselves caught in a deadly web of secrets.

The hunt leads Isla to a dangerous underground world where power-hungry vampires are turning humans into monsters. But this is only the beginning. Someone is moving in the shadows, pulling the strings, and as Isla digs deeper, she uncovers whispers of a long-buried truth, one that could shake the very foundation of the supernatural world.

The Crimson Veil is lifting, and what lies beyond it is more terrifying than she could have ever imagined.

Printed in Great Britain
by Amazon

Chapter 1: The Crimson Veil

The body lay sprawled in the alleyway, a stark contrast against the damp cobblestone. The scent of blood, thick, metallic, *wrong*, hung in the cold night air, mixing with the distant hum of city traffic. Isla Crowley crouched beside the corpse, her gloved fingers brushing the ground near the victim's outstretched hand. Something about this didn't sit right.

Not just the precision of the kill, the eerie stillness of the scene, but the absence of something she should have sensed.

"This is different," she murmured.

Camilla stood behind her, hands on her hips, scanning the surrounding alley. "Different how? Dead's dead."

Isla tilted her head. The victim, a man in his early thirties, well-dressed but unremarkable, had no obvious wounds. No gunshot, no stab marks. But the way his skin stretched tight over his bones, the unnatural paleness of his complexion, set off every alarm in her head.

"There's no blood," she said.

Camilla frowned. "What do you mean? We're standing in a damn crime scene. There's always blood."

Isla exhaled slowly, resisting the urge to state the obvious. The ground was dry. No splatter, no seepage, no pooling. It wasn't just missing; it was as if it had never been there to begin with.

She reached for her camera, snapping a few shots while keeping her instincts locked down. The last thing she needed was Camilla picking up on her unease. She wasn't ready to explain, not yet.

Camilla huffed, tapping her foot. "Okay, so let's start simple. Who is he?"

Isla pulled on her latex gloves and carefully patted down the man's jacket. A leather wallet sat snug in the inner pocket. She flipped it open.

"James Carter," she read aloud, glancing at the driver's license. "Thirty-four. Lives in Deansgate."

Camilla jotted it down. "Any family?"

A quick check through the wallet revealed a folded photo, James with a woman, possibly a wife or girlfriend, smiling at a Christmas market. Isla felt the familiar weight settle in her chest. A reminder that everybody had a life behind it.

Camilla leaned against her own desk, sipping from a coffee that had probably been sitting out for hours. "You think there's more to this than a mugging gone wrong?"

Isla hesitated, then shook her head. "Nothing was stolen. No signs of a struggle. No blood. If it was a mugging, it was the cleanest one I've ever seen."

Camilla hummed in agreement. "Alright, let's start with the basics. Home address, family, last known movements."

Typing Carter's name into the system, Isla pulled up his file. No criminal record, no outstanding debts. He worked in finance, lived in a flat near Deansgate, and,

Her fingers paused over the keyboard.

The last charge on his credit card was from The Red Veil, a bar on the outskirts of the city.

Not unusual, except for one thing.

"The last victim," Isla murmured. "David Holloway. He was at the same bar the night he died."

Camilla straightened. "So, we've got two men, both found dead under *very* weird circumstances, both last seen drinking at the same place?"

"Looks like it."

"We'll need to notify next of kin," Isla muttered, tucking the wallet into an evidence bag.

She stood, scanning the alleyway again. This wasn't random. Whoever, or *whatever*, had done this hadn't left a trace. That wasn't normal. Even the cleanest kills had something. A sign of struggle, a misplaced footprint, an indication of how the attack happened.

This?

It was like James Carter had simply, stopped being alive.

And that was the problem.

Camilla gestured to the entrance of the alley, where uniformed officers were beginning to tape off the area. "Let's wrap this up before the vultures descend."

Isla turned back to the body; her pulse steady but her instincts screaming.

This wasn't just murder.

This was something else.

Something unnatural.

And she had a feeling it was only the beginning.

that sent a chill down her spine. It was the sensation creeping along her skin, like being watched.

She turned sharply, scanning the rooftops and the dark corners beyond the tape. Nothing.

But that didn't mean they were alone.

"Isla?" Camilla's voice pulled her back.

She exhaled. "Let's get out of here."

Manchester Police Precinct – Homicide Division

The precinct was alive with the usual late-night chaos, officers coming and going, paperwork piling up, the occasional drunk being dragged in for processing. Isla had always found comfort in the hum of it all. It was normal. Predictable. A stark contrast to the world she'd left behind.

She and Camilla took the elevator up to their floor, stepping into the homicide bullpen. A few officers looked up as they passed, but most were too buried in their own cases to pay them much attention.

Sliding into her desk, Isla booted up her computer. "Let's see what we've got on James Carter."

The body was tagged, photographed, and marked for transport. Forensics had arrived, setting up their lights and evidence markers, combing through the alley for anything Isla and Camilla might have missed.

Isla stood off to the side, flipping through the victim's wallet again. James Carter. A normal man, by all appearances. No criminal record. No ties to anything shady. Yet here he was, lying in an alley, completely drained of blood.

She still hadn't said those words aloud.

Not to Camilla. Not to herself.

Because if she did, it would make it real.

Camilla finished giving instructions to the officers on site and walked back over, shoving her notebook into her coat pocket. "We need to run him through the system, see if he has any known connections, debts, or enemies."

Isla nodded, distracted. Her eyes swept the alleyway one last time. It felt... *off*. There was something missing, something she was failing to see.

The shadows stretched unnaturally long, the streetlights flickering above them. The cold pressed in, sharp and biting, but it wasn't just the temperature

"We'll need to notify next of kin," Isla muttered, tucking the wallet into an evidence bag.

She stood, scanning the alleyway again. This wasn't random. Whoever, or *whatever*, had done this hadn't left a trace. That wasn't normal. Even the cleanest kills had something. A sign of struggle, a misplaced footprint, an indication of how the attack happened.

This?

It was like James Carter had simply, stopped being alive.

And that was the problem.

Camilla gestured to the entrance of the alley, where uniformed officers were beginning to tape off the area. "Let's wrap this up before the vultures descend."

Isla turned back to the body; her pulse steady but her instincts screaming.

This wasn't just murder.

This was something else.

Something unnatural.

And she had a feeling it was only the beginning.

The body was tagged, photographed, and marked for transport. Forensics had arrived, setting up their lights and evidence markers, combing through the alley for anything Isla and Camilla might have missed.

Isla stood off to the side, flipping through the victim's wallet again. James Carter. A normal man, by all appearances. No criminal record. No ties to anything shady. Yet here he was, lying in an alley, completely drained of blood.

She still hadn't said those words aloud.

Not to Camilla. Not to herself.

Because if she did, it would make it real.

Camilla finished giving instructions to the officers on site and walked back over, shoving her notebook into her coat pocket. "We need to run him through the system, see if he has any known connections, debts, or enemies."

Isla nodded, distracted. Her eyes swept the alleyway one last time. It felt... *off*. There was something missing, something she was failing to see.

The shadows stretched unnaturally long, the streetlights flickering above them. The cold pressed in, sharp and biting, but it wasn't just the temperature that sent a chill down her spine. It was the sensation creeping along her skin, like being watched.

She turned sharply, scanning the rooftops and the dark corners beyond the tape. Nothing.

But that didn't mean they were alone.

"Isla?" Camilla's voice pulled her back.

She exhaled. "Let's get out of here."

Manchester Police Precinct – Homicide Division

The precinct was alive with the usual late-night chaos, officers coming and going, paperwork piling up, the occasional drunk being dragged in for processing. Isla had always found comfort in the hum of it all. It was normal. Predictable. A stark contrast to the world she'd left behind.

She and Camilla took the elevator up to their floor, stepping into the homicide bullpen. A few officers looked up as they passed, but most were too buried in their own cases to pay them much attention.

Sliding into her desk, Isla booted up her computer. "Let's see what we've got on James Carter."

Camilla leaned against her own desk, sipping from a coffee that had probably been sitting out for hours. "You think there's more to this than a mugging gone wrong?"

Isla hesitated, then shook her head. "Nothing was stolen. No signs of a struggle. No blood. If it was a mugging, it was the cleanest one I've ever seen."

Camilla hummed in agreement. "Alright, let's start with the basics. Home address, family, last known movements."

Typing Carter's name into the system, Isla pulled up his file. No criminal record, no outstanding debts. He worked in finance, lived in a flat near Deansgate, and,

Her fingers paused over the keyboard.

The last charge on his credit card was from The Red Veil, a bar on the outskirts of the city.

Not unusual, except for one thing.

"The last victim," Isla murmured. "David Holloway. He was at the same bar the night he died."

Camilla straightened. "So, we've got two men, both found dead under *very* weird circumstances, both last seen drinking at the same place?"

"Looks like it."

Camilla set her coffee down. "That's a lead."

It was. And a damn strong one.

Isla leaned back, drumming her fingers against her desk. There was something circling the edges of her mind, just out of reach. A pattern forming in the shadows.

She glanced at Camilla. "I think we need to pay The Red Veil a visit."

Chapter 2: The Red Veil

The Red Veil sat on the city's fringes, nestled between an abandoned textile mill and a row of forgotten warehouses. It wasn't the kind of place you stumbled into; it was the kind you sought out.

A neon-red glow bled from the sign above the entrance, humming like a heartbeat in the cold night air. The heavy bass of music throbbed through the walls, a siren's call luring in those looking to drink, disappear, or drown in something dangerous.

Isla and Camilla stepped out of the car, the pavement slick beneath their boots. The air smelled of rain, exhaust, and something richer, darker, a scent that made Isla's hackles rise.

Camilla glanced at the bouncer. "Think he'll give us trouble?"

The man standing at the door was a slab of muscle wrapped in a too-tight black shirt, eyes sharp despite the lazy way he leaned against the brick wall. He wasn't just watching people come and go, he was weighing them, deciding who was prey and who was predator.

Isla met his gaze, feeling the wolf in her stir. "Let's find out."

She walked forward, Camilla at her side, flashing her badge. "Detective Crowley, Manchester Homicide. We need to have a look inside."

The bouncer barely glanced at the badge. "We're at capacity."

Isla smiled, all teeth. "That wasn't a request."

A tense beat passed. Then the bouncer sighed, stepping aside. "Don't cause trouble."

"No promises," Camilla muttered as they stepped inside.

Inside the Red Veil

The club was a predator's dream, low lights, shadowed corners, bodies pressed together in tight, rhythmic waves. The air was thick with alcohol, sweat, and something sharper, something metallic beneath the perfume and cologne.

Blood.

The club was suffocating with heat and bodies, pulsing to the heavy bass of music that vibrated through Isla's ribs. Red light pooled in corners, casting shifting shadows across faces, distorting expressions until everyone looked like a predator waiting to strike.

The scent of sweat, liquor, and something richer, something metallic, curled around her senses. It was faint, just a whisper beneath the surface, but it was there.

Isla's gaze swept across the room. There was no sign of a struggle, no obvious marks of violence. The murder at the alley hadn't originated here, but the victim had *been* here. His last known location before he ended up dead in an ally.

Camilla nudged her. "Where do we start?"

"The bartender." Isla tilted her chin toward the long, sleek bar at the side of the club. The man behind it was wiping down a glass with a careful sort of focus, avoiding eye contact with the crowd.

They wove through the mass of people, the heat pressing against their skin. When they reached the bar, Isla flashed her badge. "Detective Crowley, MPD. We need to ask you a few questions."

The bartender, mid-thirties, shaved head, dark eyes that had seen too much, barely spared them a glance. "Busy night, Detectives."

"This won't take long," Camilla said, voice smooth but firm.

He sighed, setting down the glass. "What do you want to know?"

Isla leaned in slightly, keeping her voice low. "A man was murdered last night. We have reason to believe he was here before it happened." She slid a photo of the victim across the counter. "Do you recognize him?"

The bartender's face didn't change, but there was a flicker in his eyes, too fast to catch if she hadn't been watching.

"No," he said. Too quick. Too smooth.

"Try again."

His fingers tightened around the cloth he was holding. "I see a lot of faces."

Isla studied him. "Do you remember this one?"

A beat of silence. Then, finally, a low exhale. "He came in. Alone. Didn't say much. Ordered a drink, sat in the back."

"Did he meet anyone?"

The bartender hesitated, then shook his head. "Not that I saw."

Lying. Isla could feel it, the way his pulse ticked faster in his throat.

Camilla placed a hand on the bar, close enough that he'd feel the implied pressure. "Listen, we're trying to stop this from happening again. If you know anything, now's the time to talk."

He swallowed. His gaze flickered around the club as if checking for someone watching. Then, lowering his voice, he muttered, "He was talking to someone."

"Who?" Isla pressed.

The bartender hesitated. "A woman."

Isla and Camilla exchanged a glance.

"What did she look like?"

He wiped a hand down his face. "Dark hair. Pale. Real pale. Red dress, I think." His voice dropped lower. "She was… strange."

That metallic scent curled in Isla's nose again.

Strange.

They were on to something.

The bartender's words lingered in the thick air between them, but Isla didn't press further. Not here. Not when his fingers were already tightening around the rag as if expecting someone to come along and make him regret talking.

Instead, she slid the photo back into her coat pocket and turned to scan the club. A woman. Dark hair, red dress, pale. Not exactly a rare description, but combined with the bartender's hesitation, it was enough to set her instincts on edge.

Beside her, Camilla was already taking in the room, sharp eyes flitting across clusters of people, scanning for anyone watching them too closely. "If he's telling the truth," she murmured, "then someone in here knows her."

Isla nodded but didn't answer. Something was wrong.

It wasn't just the usual filth clinging to the edges of a place like this, the scent of old liquor and desperation woven into the walls. It was the undercurrent, the pulse beneath it all, something that made her wolf bristle beneath her skin.

There was a predator in the room.

Her muscles tightened instinctively, her senses sharpening as she let the feeling guide her gaze through the crowd. People dancing, drinking, laughing. Humans.

And then.

There.

A figure stood near the back, partially obscured by the shifting glow of neon light. Dressed in dark, well-tailored clothes, his posture too still, too composed for a place like this. And the scent rolling off him, barely masked by cologne and cigarette smoke, was wrong.

Vampire.

The realization hit her fast, her wolf snarling beneath her ribs. Not just her instincts, the knowledge of what he was settled into her bones, deep and certain.

Her first vampire.

She swallowed hard, keeping her face neutral. If she reacted, if she gave herself away, this would turn into something Camilla wasn't ready for. Wasn't supposed to be ready for.

Camilla nudged her. "Something?"

"Maybe." Isla forced herself to sound casual, tilting her head toward the far side of the club. "Let's move. See if anyone else wants to talk."

Camilla didn't question it, weaving through the crowd as Isla followed a step behind, keeping her attention split between her partner and the man in the shadows.

He was watching them now.

Not openly. Not in an obvious way. But Isla *felt* his gaze shift, felt the weight of it settle over her like a hand on the back of her neck.

He knows what I am.

Her pulse quickened.

She had to be careful. Had to get closer without drawing attention. If this was her first chance at getting answers, she couldn't waste it.

But she also couldn't let Camilla get too close.

"Hey," Isla murmured, catching Camilla's elbow as they neared the back of the club. "Why don't you see if anyone near the booths recognizes our guy? I'll check the bar."

Camilla frowned. "You sure?"

"I'll cover more ground this way." Isla offered a small, reassuring smile. "I won't go far."

A hesitation, Camilla could read her well enough to know when she was holding something back, but eventually, she nodded. "Fine. Five minutes, then we regroup."

Isla exhaled. "Five minutes."

She watched as Camilla wove toward the booths, waiting until she was fully out of earshot before shifting her focus back to the vampire.

Still watching.

Still waiting.

Isla's jaw tightened.

Fine.

She made her way toward him, steady and unhurried, every step measured. No sudden movements. No hint of nerves. Just one predator walking toward another.

The moment she was close enough, his lips curled into something that was almost a smile.

"*Little wolf*," he murmured, his voice smooth as silk. "I was wondering when you'd find me."

Chapter 3: The Devil You Know

Isla's pulse thudded against her ribs, but she didn't let it show. She had spent years learning how to hide what simmered beneath her skin, what threatened to bare its teeth when she felt cornered.

The vampire, because *that's exactly what he was*, watched her with the kind of amusement that made her want to rip his throat out. Not that she could. Not here. Not yet.

"Little wolf," he repeated, his voice smooth, edged with a knowing smirk. "You walk into my den without so much as an introduction? How *rude*."

Isla tilted her head, keeping her expression neutral. "You don't own this place."

"Don't I?" The vampire gestured lazily around them. "I own far more than you realize, Isla Crowley."

That set her teeth on edge. He knew her name. Which meant he knew *what* she was. And that? That made this a hell of a lot more dangerous.

She didn't let the unease show. Instead, she arched a brow. "I don't recall giving you my name. That's hardly fair, is it?"

The vampire's grin widened, all sharp edges and amusement. "You can call me Dorian."

Dorian. A name that carried weight, though she couldn't place why.

He took a slow sip from the glass in his hand, dark liquid swirling like wine, though Isla doubted it was. He didn't need to breathe, but he inhaled as though savouring her scent, as if tasting the air between them.

"You reek of silver and old blood," he mused. "Been playing detective, have we?"

Isla's muscles coiled.

"I'm a cop," she said flatly.

Dorian hummed. "And yet, here you are, sniffing around places a human cop would never dare."

He leaned forward, placing his drink on the table between them. The glass barely made a sound as it met the wood.

"I know why you're here, Isla."

Her spine stiffened. "Do you?"

Dorian's smile didn't waver. "You're chasing shadows. Bodies drained dry. No witnesses, no real evidence left behind. But you already *know* what's responsible, don't you?"

Her jaw clenched.

That wasn't an admission.

Dorian's chuckle was dark, pleased. "Ah. You really *are* good at this. But not good enough."

Isla didn't flinch. She met his gaze, searching for any flicker of deception. But Dorian wasn't like the others she'd hunted. He wasn't nervous. He wasn't looking for an escape. He was playing with her.

That meant he wasn't afraid.

And that? That was a problem.

"You know something," she said, voice even. "So why don't we stop wasting time?"

Dorian sighed dramatically, tapping his fingers against the glass. "So impatient. Your kind always is."

"My kind?"

His grin sharpened. "Hunters."

Isla's stomach twisted, not at the accusation, but at the way he said it. Like he knew something she didn't.

Dorian tilted his head. "Do you even know what you're hunting, little wolf?"

A flicker of something cold crawled down her spine.

"I know enough."

"No," Dorian murmured, watching her carefully. "You don't."

The way he said it, the certainty in his voice, made her pulse stutter.

He *knew* something.

Something bigger.

Something worse.

But before she could press him, before she could demand answers, his eyes flicked over her shoulder, sharp as a blade.

And then, just like that, he was gone.

Not a step, not a shift, just *vanished*.

Isla twisted, scanning the crowd, but he had melted into the shadows.

And then.

"Isla?" Camilla's voice cut through the noise, urgent.

Isla turned back just in time to see her partner pushing through the crowd, face tight.

"We have a problem," Camilla said.

"Bigger than the one that just disappeared?" Isla muttered.

Camilla's jaw clenched.

"The bartender's dead."

The noise in the club hadn't died, but it had changed. A hum of unease rippled through the patrons, voices hushed, bodies shifting toward the exits like a slow, inevitable tide.

Isla took a steadying breath, forcing her wolf to stay under control as she pushed past Camilla and moved toward the bar.

The barman, who just moments ago had been polishing glasses and giving them wary, sidelong glances, was slumped over the counter. His lifeless eyes stared ahead, lips parted as if frozen mid-breath. A single, thin trail of blood curved down from his nose to his upper lip.

No obvious wounds. No sign of a struggle.

But Isla didn't need to see puncture marks to know.

Her gut twisted.

"What the hell happened?" Camilla hissed, coming up beside her.

"We need to clear the scene," Isla said quickly. "Shut the doors. No one leaves."

Camilla nodded, her instincts kicking in despite the confusion on her face. She turned and flashed her badge, barking orders at the few bouncers by the entrance. Isla knew it wouldn't hold for long, drunken humans didn't like being told to stay put, and whoever did this might still be in the building.

Hell, Isla thought grimly, Dorian might've been sitting right next to him when it happened.

She crouched beside the body, listening, sensing. The scent of death was still fresh, warm, metallic, laced with the barest hint of something... wrong. Not just human blood.

She reached out, pressing her fingers lightly against his wrist. Cold. Too cold for someone who had been alive only minutes ago.

A human might have missed it, but Isla felt the unnatural stillness. Drained. Not entirely, not like the bodies in the alleyway, but close enough that her stomach clenched.

"Nothing obvious," she muttered, glancing up as Camilla rejoined her. "No weapon, no signs of struggle."

Camilla exhaled sharply, running a hand through her hair. "Then how the hell did he die?"

Isla didn't answer.

Because she already knew.

And if it was the same thing that had killed those bodies in the alley, then it meant one thing.

The killer was still here.

Camilla straightened. "We need to question people."

"Agreed." Isla rose to her feet, scanning the room. She locked onto a couple of bar regulars she'd seen when they first entered, ones who had been whispering as she walked past earlier.

"You take that table," she murmured, nodding toward the group by the wall. "I'll get the ones by the bar."

Camilla nodded and peeled off, already pulling out her notepad.

Isla moved to the nearest patron, a woman clutching a half-empty cocktail with nails bitten down to the quick.

"Hey," Isla said, flashing her badge. "Did you see anything?"

The woman swallowed, eyes darting to the bartender's body. "I, I don't know. He was fine, and then he just... wasn't."

"You didn't see anyone approach him?"

The woman hesitated. "There was a guy. Pale. Dark hair. Dressed real sharp. He was at the bar a minute ago."

Dorian.

Isla's stomach sank. "Where did he go?"

The woman glanced around; her face pinched. "I, he was just there."

Isla clenched her fists. No way in hell was it a coincidence.

Camilla appeared at her side, looking grim. "Nobody saw anything," she muttered. "Or they don't *want* to say anything."

Typical.

Isla glanced back toward the shadowed corners of the club. Dorian knew something. And if he ran the second the bartender dropped, it meant he wasn't working alone.

Or worse, he wasn't in control of whatever was happening.

She exhaled sharply. "We need to find him."

Camilla gave her a look. "And how do you propose we do that? He ghosted like a damn." She stopped, as if catching herself. Then sighed. "Like a damn ghost."

"He'll turn up," Isla murmured. "People like him always do."

Camilla crossed her arms. "Do I even want to know what you mean by people like him?"

Isla gave her a tight smile.

"No," she said. "You really don't."

As the wail of sirens cut through the thick Manchester night, Isla and Camilla stepped back from the crime scene. The bar was now a mess of flashing blue lights, uniformed officers cordoning off the scene where the barman's lifeless body slumped against the bar.

Detective Inspector Graves, a sharp-featured man with greying hair and permanent exhaustion in his eyes, strode towards them. "Another body, Crowley?"

he said, voice laced with irritation. "I'm starting to think you bring trouble with you."

Isla exhaled. "Yeah, well, trouble seems to have a habit of finding me first."

Graves cast a look at the corpse. "Witnesses?"

Camilla shook her head. "Not a damn one willing to talk. Everyone inside claims they 'didn't see a thing.'" She glanced at Isla, knowing full well that wasn't entirely true.

Graves sighed, rubbing his temples. "Of course. Because murder in a packed bar is *so* easy to miss." He turned back to them. "Alright, I'll take it from here. Go write up your statements and let forensics do their job."

Isla gave a curt nod. "Fine. But let me know if anything strange turns up."

Graves raised an eyebrow. "Strange how?"

Isla hesitated, then shrugged. "Just a feeling."

He snorted. "Right. Because that's useful."

Camilla looped her arm through Isla's and started steering her toward the car. "Come on, before you start a fight."

Isla didn't resist, but as they walked away, she cast one last glance at the darkened Bar. The smell of blood still lingered, and in the back of her mind, a single name echoed.

Dorian.

She didn't know why yet, but she damn well intended to find out.

Chapter 4: A Name in the Dark

Isla drove in silence, her grip tight on the steering wheel. The city lights blurred past, neon streaks cutting through the thick Manchester fog.

Camilla sat beside her, arms crossed, tapping her fingers against her thigh. She had been quiet since they left The Red Veil, but Isla knew the tension rolling off her wasn't just from the scene they had left behind.

Finally, Camilla sighed. "Alright. Enough of the cryptic bullshit, Isla. What aren't you telling me?"

Isla exhaled sharply. She hadn't wanted to do this here, but there was no more avoiding it. "I know what we're dealing with."

Camilla shot her a sharp look. "Oh? And when were you planning on sharing that with me?"

"When I was sure," Isla admitted. "But after tonight? After the bodies in the alley? After him?" She gritted her teeth. "I'm sure."

Camilla leaned forward. "Alright, then. Say it."

Isla stared ahead. "Vampires."

The word hung heavy in the air between them.

Camilla's mouth tightened. "You're serious?"

Isla nodded. "I recognised what he was the second I saw him." She hesitated. "And… I recognised his name. Dorian."

Camilla frowned. "But you don't know why?"

"No," Isla admitted. "But something about it, it's familiar." She tightened her grip on the wheel. "That's why we need to speak to Elias and Ronan."

Camilla let out a breath, shaking her head. "I can't believe we're actually saying this out loud. Vampires. *Vampires*, Isla."

"I know." Isla glanced at her. "But we don't have time to freak out about it. We need to figure out who Dorian is, what he's doing here, and how the hell we stop whoever is leaving bodies all over the city."

Camilla was silent for a moment. Then she reached for her phone. "I'll call Elias. You call Ronan."

Isla hesitated.

Camilla gave her a look. "What?"

"I don't, I didn't tell him about any of this yet."

Camilla scoffed. "You think he's not going to be pissed? He's the *Alpha*, Isla."

"I know," Isla muttered.

"Then call him," Camilla said, already dialling Elias. "Before he finds out on his own and hunts you down instead."

With a sigh, Isla pulled out her own phone, scrolling to Ronan's number.

She braced herself for the storm she was about to unleash, then pressed call.

The answer we seek

Elias' townhouse was dimly lit, the faint scent of old parchment and herbs lingering in the air. Books lined every wall, some stacked in precarious towers on the floor. The atmosphere would have been cozy if not for the weight of the conversation about to take place.

Isla stood near the fireplace, arms folded, jaw tight. Camilla had taken a seat at the worn leather couch, one leg bouncing impatiently. Elias, in his usual button-up and vest, leaned against his cluttered desk, watching them with sharp, knowing eyes.

The door swung open without warning.

"You couldn't have called?" Ronan's voice was rough with irritation as he stepped inside, his presence filling the space with authority. His sharp green eyes scanned Isla, his frustration barely masked.

"You were out of town," Isla countered. "I didn't think you'd be back this soon."

Ronan let out a breath, shutting the door behind him. "Yeah, well, when I hear you're getting tangled up with vampires, I make the trip." His gaze flicked to Camilla. "She knows?"

Camilla crossed her arms. "Considering I saw a man bled out in an alley and my partner just told me vampires are real? Yeah, I know."

Elias cleared his throat, redirecting the conversation. "We have a name," he said. "Dorian Ashford."

Ronan stilled, his expression shifting from irritation to something far darker. "Ashford?"

Isla caught the change in his demeanour immediately. "You know him?"

Ronan nodded slowly. "Old family. Dangerous family."

Elias adjusted his glasses. "Dorian is well connected in the vampire world. If he's here, it means something bigger is at play. He doesn't act without purpose."

"Well, he's definitely acting," Isla said. "He's been at the Red Veil, and he knew something about the vampire who killed the barman. I just don't know if he's trying to stop her or protect her."

Ronan exhaled sharply. "If he's protecting her, we have a bigger problem than just rogue vampires. The Ashford bloodline isn't just old, it's powerful. If he's involved in what's happening here, there's a whole hierarchy we'll have to deal with."

Camilla scoffed. "Fantastic. We barely understand the *one* vampire we've met, and now we have a whole network to worry about?"

Elias turned to Isla. "What exactly did Dorian say to you?"

She thought back to the encounter in the club, his cryptic warning, his unwavering confidence. "He called me a wolf out of my depth. He told me I didn't understand what was happening, and he made it clear that the woman we're looking for is a problem."

Ronan frowned. "That doesn't sound like a man protecting someone. It sounds like someone cleaning up a mess."

"Which means we have two problems," Elias added. "The woman turning people and Dorian, who may or may not be hunting her himself."

Camilla shook her head. "So, what now? We track down this Dorian and ask him nicely to spill his secrets?"

"No," Isla said firmly. "We track down the woman. She's the one killing people. If Dorian is after her, he'll find us soon enough."

Ronan studied her carefully. "You sure about that?"

Isla met his gaze, her wolf bristling beneath her skin. "Absolutely."

Ronan's jaw was tight as he leaned forward, forearms braced against his knees. "I've heard whispers, back in the pack, through old contacts in the underground. There's a nest in the city. Small, but growing."

"Where?" Isla asked, already feeling the adrenaline surge in her blood.

"Old industrial estate near the canals," he said. "Vacant buildings, tunnels that run deep underground. The kind of place things that don't want to be seen can thrive."

Elias exhaled sharply. "That would explain the missing persons uptick in that area." He flicked through his notes, eyes scanning data. "People disappear, and no one finds a body. It's controlled. Methodical."

Camilla's lips pressed into a thin line. "Then what are we waiting for?"

Isla nodded. "We move now."

Chapter 5: Blood in the Dark

The air was thick with the stink of rotting metal and damp concrete as Isla stepped carefully over the crumbling floor of the abandoned factory. Faint moonlight streamed through shattered windows, casting jagged shadows along the rusted machinery.

The silence was unnatural. Not just quiet, wrong. No distant city noise, no scurrying rats. Just stillness, heavy and waiting.

"I don't like this," Camilla murmured, hand resting on the grip of her gun.

Neither did Isla. Her wolf bristled beneath her skin, senses sharpening, muscles coiled.

Then she felt it.

The shift in the air.

A flicker of movement in the shadows.

Isla barely had time to snarl a warning before the first vampire struck.

It came from above, dropping from the rusted beams like a spider, claws extended, teeth bared. Isla spun, barely dodging in time, but another shape lunged from the darkness. She twisted, throwing up an arm to block a vicious strike, but claws raked across her shoulder, drawing hot blood.

Ronan was already moving. He caught one of the vampires mid-air, tackling it to the ground with a growl that echoed through the factory. His fist smashed into its face, a sickening crunch of bone.

The female vampire stepped into the dim light, her presence shifting the entire battlefield. She was tall, eerily graceful, her silver eyes glowing with amusement.

"You've been making a mess of my work," she purred, her voice as smooth as silk over a blade.

Isla bared her teeth, stance lowering into a fighter's crouch. "And you've been making a mess of my city."

The vampire only smiled. Then, with inhuman speed, she lunged.

Isla barely met the strike in time. Claws clashed, steel flashing as Isla drew a blade from her belt. The fight turned savage in seconds. The vampire was fast, too fast, but Isla had fought her kind before. She anticipated the feints, countered the strikes, ducked the deadly snap of fangs.

Then the others joined the fray.

Camilla fired, gunshots cracking through the dark, forcing one of the turned vampires to stumble back. Elias muttered an incantation, shadows twisting at his fingertips as he hurled raw energy at an attacker.

And Ronan.

Ronan was a force of nature.

He tore through them with brutal efficiency, movements precise and deadly. When Isla moved, he matched her, their strikes flowing together in instinctive, practiced rhythm.

For a moment, it was just like old times.

Then the female vampire slammed Isla against a pillar, teeth snapping inches from her throat.

"You don't even realize what you've stepped into," she whispered, her breath cold against Isla's skin. "You're fighting ghosts from a war you thought was over."

Isla drove her knee into the vampire's gut and threw her off, but the words stuck like ice in her veins.

A war that was over.

But maybe not for long.

The vampire hissed, her gaze flicking past Isla, to Ronan. Then she smiled, slow and knowing.

"I'll be seeing you, little wolf."

And then she was gone.

The remaining vampires scattered into the night, leaving only the silence, the blood, and the sinking weight of something much bigger looming just out of sight.

The silence stretched in the aftermath, thick with the scent of blood and dust. Isla's heart still pounded from the fight, her muscles coiled, waiting for another attack. But the vampires were gone, vanishing into the night like shadows slipping through the cracks.

Ronan wiped a streak of blood from his jaw, eyes still sharp and searching. "That was too easy."

Camilla scoffed, holstering her gun with a shake of her head. "*Easy?* They nearly tore us apart."

"No," Elias said, rubbing a hand over his face. "Ronan's right. That wasn't a fight. It was a warning."

Isla exhaled sharply, forcing herself to focus. The female vampire, the one pulling the strings, had been toying with them. Testing them. And now she was gone, leaving behind more questions than answers.

"We need to regroup," she said, turning to the others. "Find out who she is, what she's planning."

Ronan's mouth pressed into a thin line. "And how many more she's turned."

The thought chilled Isla. Newly turned vampires were unpredictable, feral, dangerous, and ruled by hunger. If she was building an army, it wouldn't just be the city at risk. It would be everyone.

"Let's get back to Elias's," Isla said. "We need to figure out our next move before she makes hers."

Elias didn't argue. He led the way out of the abandoned factory, the night pressing in around them as they stepped onto the empty streets.

But Isla couldn't shake the feeling that they were already being watched.

Back at Elias's House

The moment they stepped into Elias's home, he waved a hand, and the candles lining the bookshelves flared to life, casting a golden glow over the room. The scent of old parchment and herbs filled the air, a stark contrast to the blood and death they had just left behind.

Camilla collapsed onto the couch, rubbing at her temples. "Okay. Someone please tell me what the hell just happened back there."

Ronan folded his arms, his expression unreadable. "A declaration."

"From who?" Camilla asked.

Isla exhaled. "That's what we need to find out." She turned to Elias, already watching her with that calculating look of his. "You recognized her. You knew something."

Elias hesitated, then sighed, rubbing a hand over the back of his neck. "Not her specifically. But her kind."

Isla frowned. "Meaning?"

Elias moved toward his bookshelves, pulling out a thick, leather-bound volume. He flipped it open, his fingers trailing over the faded ink. "There are factions within vampire society, hierarchies, rules. Not all of them follow the same code. Some want power. Some want chaos."

He turned the book around, tapping a passage written in elegant script.

"The *Bloodbound Covenant*," Isla read aloud.

Camilla leaned forward. "That sounds ominous."

Elias nodded. "It's an old sect, one that believes in ruling from the shadows. They don't just exist within the vampire world. They control it."

Ronan's jaw tightened. "And you think she's one of them?"

Elias shook his head. "No. If she were, she wouldn't be making such a spectacle of herself. She wouldn't be openly turning humans, drawing attention. No, she's reckless. Which means she's acting alone, or at least, without permission."

Isla narrowed her eyes. "Which means she's pissing off the bigger players."

Elias met her gaze. "Exactly."

The weight of it settled in Isla's chest. This wasn't just a rogue vampire preying on the city. It was something *bigger*. Something deeper. And if they didn't stop it soon, they wouldn't just be fighting her.

They'd be fighting all of them.

A war that had ended long ago.

And now, it was starting again.

Chapter 6: The Queen's Gambit

The cavernous chamber beneath Manchester's streets reeked of damp stone and spilled blood. Flickering candlelight cast long, jagged shadows across the vaulted ceiling, illuminating the assembled figures that knelt before their queen.

Katerina stood at the head of the room, crimson eyes burning with fury. Her elegant gown was still marred with the streaks of battle, dark smears of blood where Isla Crowley's silvered blade had *cut* her. It had been *too close*.

She curled her fingers into a fist, feeling the sting of the healing wound on her ribs. The wolf had drawn blood. A slight, one that could not go unanswered.

The fight at the industrial estate had been a reckless move. She had underestimated them. Wolves, she knew how to deal with. But the warlock? The human police officer? They had complicated things.

She would not make the same mistake again.

Katerina's gaze swept across the vampires before her, her children, her army, her future. Those that had survived the ambush knelt, heads bowed in shame. Others stood against the walls, watching, waiting.

Their ranks were not yet what she had envisioned, but they were growing.

Too slowly.

Her fingers tightened at her sides.

The old ways had kept them in the dark for too long. For centuries, her kind had hidden beneath the surface, forced into the shadows by outdated laws and the threats of hunters, wolves, and warlocks alike. But the world had changed.

Manchester was a city of power. A city of blood.

And she *would* rule it.

One of her more favoured lieutenants, Marcus, stepped forward, lowering his head in deference before speaking.

"My lady, we lost too many tonight," he admitted, his voice cautious. "The wolves and their allies were prepared. They knew we were there."

Katerina's jaw tensed.

"The warlock," she murmured, her voice like silk laced with steel. "And the wolf."

The whispers about Isla Crowley had reached her ears before, but she had dismissed them. A wolf living among humans, pretending to be one of them? She had been beneath Katerina's notice.

Until tonight.

The memory of the fight burned in her mind, the way the she-wolf had moved, fought, relentless and unyielding. She was dangerous. And worse, she had help.

Elias, the warlock, had been formidable in his own way. His spells had disrupted the battlefield, had cut through her newly turned soldiers like a blade through flesh.

And that human, the woman who stood at Isla's side, the one who should have been prey, she had fought, too.

It was *insulting*.

"I want their names," Katerina said, voice smooth but laced with lethal intent. "Their histories. Their weaknesses."

Marcus hesitated. "We already know the wolf's name. Isla Crowley. She's."

"I know who she is," Katerina snapped.

Silence fell across the chamber.

She took a slow, deliberate breath.

"I want more than her name," she continued, calmer now, though the anger still simmered beneath her skin. "I want to know *what* she is. Who she answers to. Who she protects."

A smile tugged at her lips.

"She fights like a soldier. Wolves do not train their outcasts. She still has ties to her pack."

That was a weakness.

A vulnerability she could exploit.

Marcus nodded. "And the warlock?"

Katerina's eyes gleamed.

"He interests me."

Magic had always been a threat to her kind, but it had also been an asset, when wielded correctly. She had seen power in Elias' hands tonight. Controlled. Deadly. Useful.

Perhaps he could be persuaded.

Or, if not… he could be broken.

"Assemble our forces," she ordered. "Only the strongest. The rest…" Her gaze flickered to the weaker fledglings, the ones who had barely survived the night's battle. "Dispose of them."

A few of them flinched, sensing their doom.

Katerina didn't care.

She had no patience for weakness.

Her army would be built on strength, on power, on *fear*.

And when she was ready, when she had Isla Crowley at her feet and the warlock's magic in her grasp.

She would take this city.

And no one would stop her.

Chapter 7: Blood in the Streets

The metallic scent of blood still clung to Isla's skin as she and the team stood in Elias' dimly lit study. The fight at the industrial estate had been a message, *Katerina wasn't hiding anymore.*

She paced, her mind racing through everything they'd learned. The vampires they had fought were feral, turned too recently, too sloppily. That meant Katerina wasn't just building an army, she was desperate. Reckless.

Ronan leaned against the wall, arms crossed over his chest, watching her. He had that look again, the one that meant he had something to say but wasn't sure if she wanted to hear it.

Camilla sat at the desk, flipping through the case files, but her fingers drummed an anxious rhythm against the wood. She was trying to focus, but Isla could see the tension in her shoulders.

Elias, for once, was quiet. He stood by the window, staring out at the Manchester skyline like it held the answers. His magic had been drained in the fight. The bruises along his arms hadn't faded yet.

Finally, Ronan broke the silence.

"There's a nest," he said.

Isla stopped pacing. "What?"

He pushed off the wall, exhaling slowly. "I didn't want to bring it up before. Whispers, nothing confirmed. But after tonight, I'd bet my life on it."

Elias turned from the window. "Where?"

Ronan's expression darkened. "Under the city. There's a network of old tunnels, abandoned, mostly forgotten. If they're hiding a large number of fledglings, that's where they'd be."

Isla clenched her jaw. Underground. Of course. Katerina was building her army beneath their feet, and they'd been blind to it.

Camilla let out a low whistle. "Jesus. And here I thought the worst thing in Manchester's underground was the rats."

"Not just the tunnels," Ronan continued. "There's an old chapel, too. Abandoned decades ago. It's been repurposed more than once, cult meetings, drug dens. But if I had to guess?" His gaze locked onto Isla's. "That's where she is."

A chill ran through her.

Katerina was bold. She had come after them directly, had tested their strength, had let them see her face. That meant she wasn't afraid of them.

And that? *That* was a problem.

"We need to go," Isla said.

"Not yet," Elias countered.

She turned to him, frowning.

"If we charge in without a plan, we're dead," he said simply. "Vampires don't fight fair. And Katerina? She knows we're coming."

He wasn't wrong.

Isla exhaled sharply. *Think, dammit.*

They needed a strategy. They needed to draw her out, separate her from her fledglings. But how?

Camilla cleared her throat. "What if we make her come to us?"

The room fell silent.

Isla studied her partner. "Explain."

"She's been hunting in the open," Camilla said. "She's not being careful. She's turning people who aren't stable. If we make enough noise, stir things up, she won't be able to ignore us."

Elias tapped his fingers against his chin, considering. "A trap."

Ronan raised an eyebrow. "Baiting a vampire queen. That's bold, even for you."

"Yeah?" Isla rolled her shoulders. "Then let's be bold."

A slow smile spread across Ronan's face.

Elias sighed. "I'm going to regret this."

Camilla grinned. "You already do."

Hours later, in the heart of the city…

The club was alive with neon lights and pulsing bass. The kind of place where people came to disappear for a few hours, where shadows stretched long and danger lurked behind the music.

Perfect.

Isla stood at the bar, drink in hand, eyes scanning the room. She wasn't here for pleasure.

She was here for war.

Ronan was across the room, leaning against the wall, playing the part of a brooding stranger. Elias sat in a booth, pretending to nurse a drink. Camilla was at the entrance, watching every movement.

It wouldn't be long now.

They had made sure of that.

Word had spread, of a wolf sniffing around, of a hunter asking the wrong questions. The bait was set.

Now they just had to wait.

And then... the air shifted.

The temperature dropped. The music seemed to slow. Isla's wolf bristled beneath her skin.

She turned.

A figure stepped through the crowd, moving with unnatural grace. Dressed in red, lips painted the colour of fresh blood, Katerina met Isla's gaze with a knowing smile.

Game on.

Chapter 8: The Devil Wears Red

The air in the club thickened the moment Katerina stepped through the doors.

Isla's body reacted before her mind caught up, muscles tight, heart rate spiking, senses blazing with the wild, primal recognition of a predator entering her space. Every instinct screamed danger, but she held her ground.

Katerina didn't approach quickly. She didn't need to. She strolled through the crowd like she owned it, like she *owned* them. Humans shifted unconsciously out of her path, eyes glossing over, charmed by her presence without ever realizing it. Compulsion was thick in the air, woven through every gesture, every calculated smile.

This was power, and it was being wielded without restraint.

From across the room, Ronan straightened, his eyes locked on the vampire. His wolf was just under his skin too, Isla could sense it in the taut lines of his posture, in the faint golden shimmer in his irises. He was ready to spring.

Not yet. Not until we know what she wants.

Elias moved subtly in the booth, muttering something under his breath. Protective wards, most likely. His magic vibrated faintly in the atmosphere, clashing with the thick fog of compulsion.

Katerina reached the bar and, without a word, slid into the empty stool beside Isla.

Her perfume was rich and old, something ancient and decadent, like dried roses and iron.

"You wear your power well," she said, her voice like velvet draped over steel. "But you haven't earned it yet."

Isla didn't look at her. "You're bold, showing up like this."

"I prefer fearless," Katerina said. "And I came to talk, not to fight."

Isla took a slow sip of her drink, eyes on the mirror behind the bar. Katerina had no reflection.

Noted.

"Is that what the bodies are?" Isla asked coldly. "Conversation starters?"

Katerina chuckled. "Collateral. You'd be amazed how messy progress can be."

"Progress." Isla turned to look at her fully. "You're turning people who can't handle it. You're creating monsters."

"They're only monsters because they don't understand what they're becoming," Katerina said, unbothered. "I offer freedom. Power. A new order."

"A bloodbath," Isla countered.

Katerina's smile curled. "We're not so different, you and I. You left your pack, carved your own path. Tell me that wasn't about power."

Isla's jaw tightened. "I walked away to protect them. Not to rule over them."

Katerina leaned in, her voice low and silken. "Then you'll be the first to fall."

Behind Isla, Ronan was already moving.

Too late.

Katerina vanished in a blur of speed.

Shouts erupted. Tables crashed. The crowd panicked.

The next second, a blast of force threw Isla across the room. She rolled, landed on her feet, claws out. Ronan lunged from the opposite side of the club, snarling mid-shift. Camilla shouted something, trying to push civilians toward the exits.

Elias stood in the centre of the chaos, chanting with rapid urgency, his eyes glowing faintly blue. He threw up a barrier just as Katerina reappeared, fangs bared, hands like claws.

The shield crackled as she struck it.

"You're clever," she hissed. "But clever isn't enough."

Isla launched herself forward, claws aimed for Katerina's throat.

The vampire twisted, caught her mid-air and slammed her into the ground. Pain exploded in Isla's ribs, but she kicked upward, catching Katerina in the gut and sending her staggering back.

Ronan was there in a heartbeat, his claws sinking into her side. Katerina shrieked, grabbed his throat, and hurled him into the bar with enough force to splinter the counter.

Camilla fired a round from her sidearm, it hit, but barely staggered the vampire.

Elias shouted, the final word of a spell igniting in the air.

A blast of light erupted from his hands, sending Katerina reeling. Smoke curled from her skin.

She hissed, vanishing again in a blur, this time out the door.

Silence fell, broken only by the crackle of Elias' fading magic.

The club was in ruins. Bodies moaned, dazed but alive. Ronan groaned from the wreckage of the bar.

Isla slowly stood, shaking, blood on her hands and fire in her veins.

"She's not afraid of us," Camilla said, breathless, stunned.

"No," Isla said, staring at the broken doorway.

"But she should be."

Chapter 9: Smoke and Blood

Katerina stormed into the underground tunnels beneath the city like a bullet trailing smoke. The scent of scorched flesh clung to her skin, a reminder of Elias' magic, old magic, sharper than it had any right to be in this modern age. She didn't bleed like mortals, but the pain licked along her ribs all the same.

She'd underestimated them.

That won't happen again.

The tunnels were ancient, built in the 1800s and long since forgotten by the humans who paved the streets above. The scent of rot and damp stone welcomed her like an old friend. The flicker of oil lamps lined the passageways now, her touch, her domain. These tunnels were her home, her nest. Her kingdom.

And tonight, her pride was wounded.

Two of her turned ones, Vince and Rhea, stood waiting in the stone chamber ahead, their eyes wide as she entered. They could feel her fury before she said a word.

"She's a wolf," Katerina hissed, pacing the floor. "The one in the club. A shifter, *of all things*." She wiped blood from her jaw, the scent of it thick with adrenaline. "And not just any shifter, she fights like an Alpha."

"You said she was just a detective," Vince said cautiously.

"I said she was hiding in plain sight." Katerina's voice was a whip. "There's a difference."

She spun toward the far wall where a hand-drawn map of Manchester was pinned to the crumbling stone. She pressed a finger to a circle etched in red ink, the bar, the industrial estate, a string of dots trailing through the city. There was no pattern, not yet, but the chaos she'd unleashed had stirred every corner of the supernatural world.

That was the point.

"They're not ready for a war," she said softly, more to herself than the others. "They've grown lazy. Peace makes fools of predators."

Rhea approached, eyes glowing faintly gold in the lamplight. "You said you wanted to rule quietly. Build your court. Now you're provoking the wolves, *and* the witches."

"I'm being challenged," Katerina snapped. "By a mutt and her merry band of misfits."

A pause.

"She doesn't even know who she's really dealing with."

Vince swallowed. "And Dorian?"

Katerina's eyes narrowed. "Still playing the loyal lapdog, no doubt. Watching. Judging. But he hasn't moved against me."

"Yet," Rhea said.

Katerina smiled, an icy, humourless thing. "If he had any real authority, he'd have done it by now. No, he's afraid. They all are. I'm the future of this city, and I won't be kept in the shadows any longer."

She turned back to her map, fingers dragging down to the canals, the underground crypts, and finally... the red mark that sat at the centre of it all.

"I want more turned," she ordered. "But no more from the clubs. That's too visible. Go to the camps, the shelters, the fringes. Find the broken ones. The ones no one will miss."

"And if they don't survive the turning?" Vince asked.

Katerina didn't even flinch. "Then they weren't worthy."

"What do you think?" Camilla asked quietly, crouching beside her.

Isla didn't answer right away. Her gaze swept the alley, no signs of a struggle, no footprints beyond the ones already marked by evidence tags. Just like the last two.

"Same pattern," she murmured. "No witnesses. No CCTV. In and out like ghosts."

"Or something faster," Camilla muttered.

Isla's lips twitched in agreement. "Or stronger."

She stood, glancing up at the row of apartments facing the alley. "Get someone to canvas those flats. Anyone who heard or saw anything unusual overnight. Even the smallest detail. A noise, a shadow, a face."

Camilla nodded and moved off.

As Isla turned away from the body, her phone buzzed. A message from Elias.

We need to talk. Now. They're escalating.

She slipped the phone away and forced her face into a mask of professional calm as Chief Inspector Maddox arrived on the scene, his heavy coat soaked from the drizzle and his eyes already narrowed.

"Detective Crowley," he said gruffly. "Three bodies in a single day? You want to tell me what the hell is going on in my city?"

Isla met his gaze evenly. "We're working with the theory it's a new synthetic drug. Something powerful and untraceable so far. Possibly black market. We've sent samples to the lab for tox reports."

Maddox snorted. "This doesn't look like any drug I've ever seen."

You have no idea.

"We're also pulling links between the victims," Isla continued smoothly. "All young men. All last seen in or around the northern quarter. We're mapping their movements, checking digital footprints. We'll find the source."

He grunted, unconvinced. "And the press?"

"We're keeping it contained. Accidental overdoses for now. Until we know more."

Maddox stared at her for a beat too long. Isla held her breath, just a fraction, and then he nodded, turned, and barked orders at the uniformed officers behind him.

Camilla returned, slipping in beside her.

"He's not buying it," she whispered.

"He doesn't need to," Isla said quietly. "He just needs to think I am."

Camilla frowned. "How long do we keep lying?"

"As long as it takes."

They walked back toward the car in silence. As soon as the doors were shut, Isla pulled out her phone again and texted Elias back.

Meet us. Safe house, one hour. Bring Ronan.

They had to move. Fast. Katerina was growing bolder, more reckless. The bodies weren't just a message anymore, they were the start of something.

And Isla could feel it in her blood:
The real war was about to begin.

Camilla leaned forward over her desk, the harsh glow of the overhead lights washing her face in an exhausted pallor. A scatter of files lay open before her, photos, police reports, interview notes. A steaming cup of cheap station coffee sat untouched by her elbow, long since gone cold.

"They're not connected by family, or work, or school," she muttered, more to herself than to Isla, who stood at the board across the room, pinning up the latest victim's photo. "But all of them were drawn to that same area. The bars, the alleyways... the shadows."

Isla kept her back to Camilla, jaw tight. "That's the only link we've got. The Red Veil and the clubs near it. They didn't know each other. They were chosen."

Camilla swivelled in her chair. "Chosen by who? We can't exactly write 'lured by vampire mind control' in the case file."

"No. But we can start mapping their movements before they died." Isla turned; eyes sharp. "Find out who they spoke to. Who they flirted with. Who followed them out."

Camilla grabbed the file closest to her. "Victim one, Liam Brooks. Phone data says he matched with someone on a dating app the night he died. But the account was deleted the next day."

"Same with victim two," Isla said grimly. "Whoever's behind this is covering their tracks. Wiping digital footprints."

"I'll put in a request to the cyber crimes unit, see what they can dig out of the server logs."

"We'll need to plant a reason why." Isla crossed the room, voice low. "Say we think the victims were catfished by a black-market dealer pushing that hypothetical drug. That'll give them enough to go on."

Camilla hesitated, then nodded. "It's a good enough lie. For now."

A knock sounded on the office door. A young officer stuck his head in.

"Detectives, body from earlier has been moved to the morgue. Coroner's running tox screens now. I'll bring you the report as soon as it lands."

"Thanks," Isla said, and waited for the door to click shut before looking back at Camilla.

"I'm done spinning wheels here. Let's go."

Camilla pushed back from the desk. "Safe house?"

Isla nodded once. "It's time we got answers. From people who won't blink when we say the V-word."

The safe house was tucked into a quiet corner of the city's outskirts, masked by a shuttered bakery front. Inside, the scent of burnt sage clung to the walls, woven with the older, deeper smell of salt and silver. Protection magic, old and enduring. The city had its secrets, and so did those who defended it.

Ronan was already there, pacing like a caged wolf, tension wound through every line of his frame. Elias sat nearby, a book open in his lap, but his fingers had stopped moving across the pages.

"You're late," Ronan growled as Isla and Camilla stepped inside.

"We're buried in bodies," Isla said flatly, slamming the door behind her. "And we're out of time."

She threw the latest photos onto the table. Elias's face paled as he looked them over.

"Same pattern," he muttered. "No visible wounds. No blood left. But these aren't clean kills anymore. They're fast. Sloppy."

"She's losing control," Isla said. "Or she's turning more than she can manage."

Ronan's brows knit. "*She?*"

"Katerina," Elias supplied. "She's turned at least half a dozen humans that we know of. Probably more. Most of them are volatile, unstable. Some burn out within days. Others…" His eyes flicked to the photos. "They feed. And they kill."

"Dorian hinted she's acting outside the bounds," Isla added. "That she's not sanctioned by whatever hierarchy governs them."

Ronan leaned forward, hands braced on the table. "That means she's a liability. To them as well as to us."

Camilla frowned. "So why haven't they taken her out themselves?"

"Maybe they don't know yet," Elias said.

"Or maybe," Isla said darkly, "they're watching. Waiting to see how far she goes. And if we become a problem in the process."

Silence fell. Thick. Electric.

Then Ronan spoke, voice low. "There's another nest. A quiet one. Old. Rumours put it beneath the foundations of the old theatre near Castlefield. If Katerina's stepped outside their rule, they might know about it."

Isla looked at him, eyes hard. "You think they'll talk?"

"They might. To you."

Isla clenched her jaw. "Then I guess we pay them a visit."

And somewhere beneath the streets of Manchester, another plan was already taking shape.

The hunt was far from over.

Chapter 11: Beneath the Stone

The rain hadn't let up for hours, Manchester's sky weeping down over the cobbled streets and the winding canals of Castlefield. Isla stood at the edge of the old Roman fort remains, hands tucked into her coat pockets, the scent of wet stone and ancient earth thick in her nostrils. Streetlights glimmered on puddles. Tourists were long gone.

"This is the spot?" Camilla asked, stepping beside her, glancing around at the quiet ruins.

Isla nodded. "Oldest part of the city. Long before the Romans, even. Places like this... they remember things. Hide things."

Behind them, Elias and Ronan approached, their boots echoing off the slick stone paths.

"There's a passage," Elias said, pointing toward the crumbling archway of a once-grand subterranean theatre entrance, now sealed off to the public by rusting iron gates. "Not many know about it. Fewer still dare go down."

Ronan rolled his shoulders. "We're not most people."

With practiced ease, Ronan bent the lock with a grunt, and the gate creaked open. The four slipped inside, torches flicking to life as Elias pulled out an enchanted flare, a soft green light pulsing like a heartbeat.

They descended.

Old stairs spiralled down into damp shadow. Moss covered stone. Faint markings carved into the walls, some Roman, some older, half-erased by time.

Isla felt it first.

That stillness in her gut. A prickling awareness along her skin.

"Wards," she murmured. "Faint. Old. Still active."

"They don't want to be found," Elias said softly.

As they reached the bottom, a vast chamber unfolded before them. Rows of broken seats curved inward like ribs around a stage long rotted to dust. And standing in the centre, silent, unmoving, was a man.

Or something like one.

He was pale, skin stretched too tightly over angular bones. Clothes centuries out of date, dusted with grime. His eyes opened slowly as the group approached, black as pitch.

"Visitors," he said, voice brittle with disuse.

Isla stepped forward. "We seek information."

"Many do," he replied. "Few leave with it."

Ronan tensed beside her, fists clenched at his sides.

"We don't need much," Isla said carefully. "A woman, Katerina. She's making moves above ground. Turning humans. Causing chaos."

The ancient vampire didn't blink. "We are aware."

"So, do you condone it?"

A long pause.

"She is… ambitious."

"That's one word for it," Camilla muttered under her breath.

"She does not speak for us," he continued. "Nor does she follow the paths we honour. But she is not ours to answer for."

"Then whose is she?" Elias asked, stepping beside Isla.

Another pause. And then, just a faint, ghosting smile.

"You hunt shadows," the vampire said. "And forget how vast the night truly is."

The words chilled Isla more than the air down there ever could.

Ronan stepped forward. "We're not here to start a war. But if one comes to us, we won't stand down."

The old vampire inclined his head. "Then tread carefully, Alpha. What wakes now has slept long, and its hunger is not easily sated."

The air shifted. The room grew colder. And Isla knew the conversation was over.

They turned without another word, retreating up the winding stairs.

Outside, the city's noise returned like a crashing tide, horns, footsteps, wind against stone. But none of them spoke for a long while.

Only when they reached the safe house again did Elias finally break the silence.

"They're not protecting her. But they're not stopping her either."

"She's operating without permission," Isla said. "But she's not the threat they care about."

Camilla looked between them. "Then who do they care about?"

No one answered. Because the real answer was still sleeping. And it wouldn't stay that way forever.

Chapter 12: Blood on the Tracks

The body count was rising.

Two more in the last twenty-four hours, both young men, found in the backstreets behind Piccadilly Station. Their throats torn, eyes wide in frozen terror. No blood left in their bodies.

The press was eating it up. The city was starting to panic. And Isla was running out of time.

"Surveillance picked up movement near the abandoned rail yard just before midnight," Camilla said, sliding a photo across the table. "This grainy piece of nothing is the best we've got."

Isla studied the image. A shadowed figure crouched in the corner of a derelict platform, barely more than a blur. But her senses prickled. The stance was off. Too low. Too predatory.

"He's still out there," Isla said. "One of Katerina's, but feral. He didn't turn right. Which means he's sloppy. Dangerous."

Ronan crossed his arms. "That also makes him traceable. Feral ones leave trails."

Elias nodded. "He'll be feeding often. Lashing out. If we track the scent from the scene, we might get lucky."

"I'll take the lead," Isla said, already rising. "He's mine."

The old railway district was a corpse of rusted metal and crumbling platforms. Fog hung low between the disused tracks, coiling through broken train cars and shattered windows.

Isla crouched near the most recent kill site, pressing her fingers to a sticky patch of earth.

Still warm.

The scent hit her like a blow, blood, rot, rage. And something sharp beneath it. Wrong.

"He's close," she whispered, eyes flashing gold for the briefest moment.

Camilla stood back, gun drawn. Ronan flanked them silently, his presence a steadying force. Elias held a faint charm in one hand, murmuring under his breath, watching for movement.

Then they heard it.

A low, guttural growl.

From the shadows beneath a twisted support beam, the feral vampire leapt.

He was half-naked, skin mottled grey, eyes wild and burning red. He moved too fast for a human, too erratically for one of the well-turned. His body smashed into Isla like a train, sending her sprawling.

She hit the ground, rolled, and came up with her silver blade drawn. The vampire screeched and lunged, only for Ronan to crash into him from the side, slamming him against the rusted train car with a bone-crunching *thud*.

"You stink of weakness," Ronan growled.

The feral hissed and clawed, managing to slice Ronan's shoulder before Elias muttered a sharp incantation. The vampire froze mid-lunge, body seizing up, long enough for Isla to drive her blade through his shoulder and pin him to the ground.

Blood sprayed, dark and thick.

"Hold him!" Isla snapped, straddling the creature as he thrashed.

"Where's your maker?" she demanded, pressing the blade closer. "Where's Katerina?"

The feral just snarled, snapping his teeth.

"Isla." Camilla warned.

Then his mouth opened wide, far too wide. A scream erupted from his throat, deafening and inhuman. Not just pain.

A warning. *To her.*

And then his body convulsed, black veins rippling under his skin, and he began to burn. From the inside out. Fire that wasn't fire, eating him from beneath the flesh. Within seconds, there was nothing left but ash and bone.

"Holy shit," Camilla whispered.

"He was silenced," Elias said grimly. "She didn't want him talking."

Ronan wiped the blood from his arm. "She knows we're hunting. And she's not playing anymore."

Later That Night

The skyline of Manchester gleamed with false calm as rain returned to the city's skin. Across the rooftops, a new storm was brewing and in a decaying ballroom hidden beneath an abandoned hotel near Deansgate, Katerina paced before her gathered fledglings, those few who had survived her turning.

The ones with enough strength to hold her power.

"She grows bold," she hissed, tossing a goblet of blood against the stone wall. It splattered like paint.

"Crowley," she snarled. "Her name is like poison in my mouth."

Behind her, two more vampires knelt, freshly turned, still weak.

"She's tasted my scent. Touched one of mine. That cannot be allowed."

One of her lieutenants stepped forward. "Let us finish her."

Katerina turned slowly, eyes glowing bright crimson. "No. *I* will finish her. But first…"

She lifted her hand, and from the shadows came more of her creations. Feral, wild-eyed things twisted by incomplete turning.

"Release them," she ordered. "Let the city feel what it means to deny me. Let her chase corpses while I take what's mine."

The ballroom shook with the shrieks of hunger.

And above, in the city of rain and stone, the hunt was only just beginning.

Chapter 13: The First Culling

Rain slammed against the city like war drums, soaking stone, glass, and steel in a sheet of cold fury. Sirens howled in the distance, blending with the unnatural shrieks that had begun piercing the night. Manchester was bleeding, and only a few knew why.

Isla hit the pavement hard, her boots skidding as she turned the corner into the edge of Northern Quarter. The air was thick with smoke, screams, and the copper tang of blood.

"They're everywhere," Camilla shouted over the chaos, ducking behind an overturned bench. "We've got five, maybe six sightings in this district alone!"

Isla could barely keep track of the movement, feral vampires darted through alleys, scaling walls, latching onto victims before melting back into the shadows. They didn't kill clean. These ones tore flesh, fed like animals. It was chaos incarnate.

"Don't engage alone," Isla growled into her comms. "We regroup at the cathedral square, Elias, I need you now."

"I'm prepping a containment ward," Elias' voice crackled through. "Don't let any of them leave the district. We'll bottleneck them there."

"I'll clear your path," Ronan said from another channel, his voice all gravel and battle lust.

Suddenly, a feral lunged at Isla from above, dropping from a broken balcony like a bag of bones. She turned just in time, planting her knife deep into its chest as they both slammed to the ground. It writhed under her, snarling until she twisted the blade and its body stilled.

She rolled off, panting, her hands slick with dark blood.

Three more came barrelling down the street toward them.

Ronan exploded into the fray from the shadows, shifting mid-leap. His wolf form hit the first feral like a freight train, snapping its spine in one violent motion. Fur matted with blood, teeth bared, he turned on the next with a guttural growl that sent the creature fleeing straight into Isla's blade.

The third, more coordinated than the others, grabbed Camilla and slammed her against the wall.

Isla's heart stopped.

But Camilla didn't hesitate.

Silver rounds spat from her sidearm, punching into the vampire's chest. It screamed and dropped her just as Ronan tackled it from behind, jaws ripping into its throat.

Camilla slid to the ground, coughing, but alive. "Okay. That was too close."

"You good?" Isla pulled her up.

Camilla nodded, eyes wide. "Better with you here."

They moved, the three of them, wolf, hunter, and warrior, clearing the street like a well-oiled machine. More police were arriving, pushing civilians back, setting up barriers. Isla flashed her badge and barked orders, hiding the truth behind the guise of a "gang attack" and "drugs gone wrong."

Only a few on the force knew better. And they didn't ask questions.

Elias arrived moments later, coat flaring as he stepped into the centre of the square, ancient symbols glowing faintly on his hands. He drove a silver stake into the wet stone and began chanting.

The ground pulsed.

"I need two minutes!" he called.

"We'll buy you five!" Isla shouted back.

The ferals surged again.

They came from rooftops, sewers, broken windows. Twenty, maybe more. Claws and fangs. Uncoordinated, feral, but overwhelming in number.

Ronan shifted back to human form mid-run, blood dripping down his arm, blade in hand. "Stay close to me."

"Never planned on doing otherwise," Isla said grimly, slamming a stake through the eye socket of a snarling vampire.

Camilla flanked them, her silver-laced baton cracking skulls, bullets whizzing.

The fight became a blur of blood and motion, Isla ducking, slicing, shoving ferals into silver barriers Elias had flung up like invisible traps. Ronan moving like a whirlwind of muscle and fury. Camilla, her fear buried beneath sheer grit, covering their flanks with surgical precision.

Then.

A scream pierced the air, different from the others.

One of the ferals burst into flame, set alight by the sealing spell Elias finished with a roar.

A dome of blue-white energy pulsed across the cathedral square, locking the remaining ferals inside.

"Now!" Elias shouted. "End them!"

And they did.

It was a massacre.

Blade met flesh, silver seared, and claws tore. The air was thick with smoke, ash, and the stench of death. When the last one fell, twitching in the rising mist, Isla stood among the bodies, heaving for breath.

They had won.

But it didn't feel like victory.

Not when civilians had died. Not when this was only the beginning.

She looked to Ronan, covered in blood, breathing heavily.

To Elias, drained, leaning against the warding post.

And to Camilla—still standing. Still fighting.

"Katerina did this," Isla whispered.

"And she'll do worse," Elias said grimly. "Tonight was a test."

Isla sheathed her blade. "Then we'll give her the answer."

The aftermath was always worse.

Smoke curled in lazy spirals above the cathedral square, the scent of burned flesh and gunpowder thick in the air. Rain hadn't washed the blood away yet, it pooled in broken cobbles and ran down cracked gutters like red ink, painting the story no one was allowed to tell.

Isla's boots were slick as she walked between the fallen, her blade still wet. Every step reminded her just how close it had been. Camilla jogged up beside her, eyes scanning, hands trembling just slightly.

"We've got civilians down on the east side. Two still breathing. I called it in as a synthetic drug reaction, unregulated compound, violent psychosis, hallucinations. The medics are buying it… so far."

Isla nodded, her jaw tight. "Keep the pressure on that story. If anyone asks, we're dealing with a tainted batch of something new. Call it *Crimson Ice* or whatever the hell sounds edgy enough to scare the press."

Nearby, a forensics team in hazmat suits began tagging the dead. Isla moved quickly, crouching beside a body still smoking from Elias' spell, fangs half-exposed, inhuman eyes rolled back. She yanked a black tarp from the back of a van and covered it.

"Cam, help me swap these tags. The ones with puncture wounds to the neck, clawed victims, mark them as civilian. Anyone with deformities, sharp teeth, or too much healing damage, perps. Say they were found in a state of overdose-fuelled aggression."

"You're asking me to lie to our entire department," Camilla muttered under her breath as she grabbed another tag. "Again."

"I'm asking you to keep us in our jobs. And the city calm."

"I know." Camilla sighed, snapping the new tag into place. "It's just getting harder. Lying, I mean. To them. To myself."

Isla glanced at her, softer now. "You're doing what most couldn't. You've stepped into the dark with us and you haven't flinched. That counts for something."

Camilla gave a dry laugh. "I'm flinching on the inside, believe me."

They continued their grim work. As more ambulances arrived, Isla directed paramedics to specific survivors, those mauled by ferals but alive. No bites. She couldn't risk an accidental turning.

Ronan approached, shirtless and blood-streaked, his arm wrapped in gauze. "I've sent two of my pack to shadow the ambulances. Make sure none of the injured try to rise mid-transport."

"Appreciated," Isla said.

"And Elias?" Camilla asked, glancing around.

"Burned himself out again," Ronan grunted. "He's on his feet but he's pale and pissy. He's taking shelter at the safehouse to recharge."

"Good. We'll regroup there soon."

But first, they had to control the narrative.

Isla moved toward the nearest police sergeant, pulling her ID from her coat and flipping to the task force seal Elias had enchanted to give her clearance. "Sergeant, I need a full lockdown on this zone. All digital uploads from bodycams, phones, anything civilian, flagged for review. This scene is a Class Three chemical event. Public Health is going to be crawling all over this by morning."

The sergeant blinked, clearly unsure, but the symbol glowed faintly, influencing just enough.

"Yes, ma'am. We've already started sweeping devices."

"Good. Mark this as a synthetic narcotic incident. Focus your statement on hallucinogenic effects, animalistic behaviour, violent outbreaks. Any chatter about monsters or supernatural crap, dismiss it as panic and mass hysteria."

"Understood."

As the officer stepped away to issue orders, Isla turned back to her team. "We've got maybe twelve hours before someone starts asking the wrong questions. We need to hit that safehouse and figure out what the hell this was. That many ferals in one coordinated assault? This wasn't desperation. It was strategy."

"Or sacrifice," Ronan muttered, eyes narrowing.

Camilla looked up. "You think Katerina sent them to die?"

Isla exhaled slowly. "I think she sent them to test us. To stretch us thin. And next time… she'll bring more."

Ronan's voice was low and hard. "Then we'll be ready."

Isla glanced once more at the bloodied square, the stained stones of the cathedral, the flashing blue lights washing the dead in cold hues.

They were barely holding this together.

But she'd hold it as long as it took.

"Let's move."

Chapter 14: The Gathering Storm

The safehouse sat tucked between two crumbling textile warehouses on the edge of Ancoats, old industrial bones hiding a living secret. From the street, it looked like little more than a disused storage facility with boarded-up windows and rusted steel doors. But beneath the grime and cracked bricks, wards shimmered, subtle and strong, layers of protection woven by Elias over the years.

Inside, the air was cooler, humming with residual magic. The walls were thick, soundproofed, reinforced with wolf-strength concrete and vampire-resistant steel. Every inch had been reinforced after one too many midnight raids.

Isla pushed the door open with her shoulder and let the others follow in behind her. Elias was already waiting, leaning against the large worktable in the middle of the main room, a mug of black coffee steaming in his hand and exhaustion in the sharp lines of his face.

"You look like hell," Camilla said, dropping into the battered leather armchair.

Elias didn't argue. "You try blocking half a dozen ferals and a shadow beast with a ward stone held together by dried blood and spite."

"You lived," Ronan muttered, slamming the door shut behind him. "We've seen worse."

"True," Elias replied, pushing himself off the table. "And we're about to see worse yet."

Isla moved toward him. "What have you got?"

He pulled a manila folder from beneath a stack of ancient books and tossed it onto the table. "I've been digging into old vampire migration records. Quiet rumours. Forgotten lines. There's one name that keeps coming up around any mention of rising ferals or blood cults."

Camilla leaned in. "Let me guess. Katerina?"

Elias nodded. "She's been in and out of Europe for decades, always on the periphery. Never enough to stir suspicion. But she's not a nobody, Isla. She's old. Like *ancient*. Some records trace her back to the Thirty Years' War. She was a high-ranking soldier during the Vampire Accord conflicts. Disappeared when the ceasefire was signed."

"And now she's back," Isla muttered.

"She was once part of a vampire court in Eastern Europe," Elias went on. "But she went rogue. Believed vampires should rule outright, not hide in the shadows. She's a purist, maybe even a supremacist. Believes in bloodlines. Strength through power."

"She thinks she's untouchable," Ronan said grimly.

"Because she's close," Elias added. "To something. Or *someone*."

Isla frowned. "What do you mean?"

"I've been following traces of magical blood signatures in the victims' autopsies," Elias said, pulling out another page. "Whatever she's doing, she's trying to amplify the turning process. But it's not working. Some of the ferals we fought tonight, they weren't just new, they were unstable. Too fast. Too hungry."

"She's trying to build an army," Isla said.

"And it's failing," Camilla added. "Which means she'll keep pushing harder."

Ronan's eyes burned amber. "Then we find her before she figures it out."

Isla nodded, pacing the room. "She's pushing into new feeding grounds. Targeting vulnerable areas. But she's got bigger ambitions, this isn't just about power."

Elias lowered his voice. "She's after a seat at the table. And she's doing it *without* the permission of the vampire hierarchy."

"Which means they'll come for her eventually," Isla said, "but not before she wrecks half the city."

A tense silence settled. Then Camilla stood.

"So, what do we do next?"

Isla exhaled, her voice steady. "We track the next body. The next turning. She's drawing power from the fear and chaos. We hit back harder. Fast. Quiet. If we can take one of her inner circle alive…"

"We make them talk," Ronan finished.

Elias moved to the wall and pulled down a battered city map, marking fresh red pins along a crescent that cut through Castlefield, Ancoats, and Deansgate.

"She's tightening her grip here. Feeding in small clusters. We've got to split up. Cover more ground. Look for irregular movement, vanishings, sudden deaths, club fires, blood trails with no attackers."

Isla nodded slowly. "Then it starts tonight. No more waiting."

But across the city, Katerina watched from the top floor of a glass-and-marble skyscraper, her false reflection flickering in the window as she sipped from a crystal glass filled with deep crimson.

"Let them hunt," she whispered. "Let them sweat."

Behind her, a man knelt, newly turned, trembling, blood on his lips. A city council pin still glinting on his jacket.

"My army rises," she said, eyes blazing. "And the throne is waiting."

Chapter 15: The Blood Trail

The city never truly slept.

Even in the dead hours, when the clubs bled out their final patrons and streetlights flickered like dying stars, Manchester pulsed with the uneasy rhythm of something ancient stirring beneath its surface.

Rain slicked the pavements in Castlefield, turning cobblestones into mirrors. Isla crouched beside a rusted storm drain behind an abandoned pub. The scent hit her before her fingers touched the puddle beside it, metallic, sour, old.

"Blood," she whispered, glancing up at Camilla who stood a few feet away, flashlight sweeping the alley.

Camilla grimaced. "You sure it's not just piss and rotten kebab?"

"I'm a wolf, remember?" Isla stood, brushing her fingers clean against her jeans. "This was human. Not old either, maybe four hours. And laced with fear."

Camilla stiffened. "Another body?"

"Not yet. But someone ran through here. And they were being hunted."

They were following the eastern edge of the blood crescent Elias had marked, an arc of violent incidents forming a crescent-shaped pattern across the city. He believed it was Katerina's feeding zone, expanding steadily outward. The goal tonight was to pressure her forces, draw out ferals, find patterns, leave no stone unturned.

Camilla muttered into her radio. "Unit 3, check the old meatpacking plant on Water Street. We're moving east."

The comms crackled. "Copy. No movement yet."

"Let's check the tram yard," Isla said, pointing ahead. "It's a bottleneck. If someone ran, they might've tried to get into the tunnels."

The two moved in silence, Isla's senses prickling at every sound. The hum of distant traffic. The buzz of neon signs. The whisper of wind that sounded too much like breath.

She paused. Something was off.

"Cam," she murmured.

Camilla stopped. "What?"

"Behind us."

Camilla pivoted just in time to catch the blur of motion, something snarling, sprinting across the rooftops.

"MOVE!"

The creature leapt, crashing into crates where they'd stood a second before. Isla rolled, teeth bared, and came up with her blade drawn, silver alloy gleaming in the low light. The feral vampire crouched on all fours, body twisted with imperfect transformation, eyes wild and red.

Isla didn't hesitate.

She surged forward, blade slashing in a downward arc. The creature hissed, dodging right, only to catch Camilla's stun baton across the face. It stumbled, shrieking, but didn't fall.

"Go for the heart!" Isla shouted.

Camilla struck again, this time sending a burst of electricity through its neck. It spasmed, long enough for Isla to drive the blade into its chest.

The body crumpled, convulsing violently. Then, stillness.

"God," Camilla breathed, panting. "That's the third one tonight."

"Four," Isla corrected, wiping the blade. "We need to call it in."

Camilla pulled out her phone but paused, frowning. "Isla… look."

The body was dissolving, decaying rapidly, skin blackening and shrinking as if the magic sustaining it was being pulled back.

"She's losing control," Isla whispered. "They're unstable. They're dying too fast."

Before they could react, the radio crackled again, Ronan's voice, sharp and clipped.

"Warehouse district. Five confirmed ferals. Elias is injured. I'm holding them off."

Isla didn't wait.

"Let's move."

In the heat of the rush

Blood soaked the concrete floor, thick and black.

Ronan stood between Elias and the remaining two ferals, fangs bared, claws extended. His shirt was torn, his side already healing from a deep gash across his ribs.

"You two are ugly enough to be hers," he growled.

The ferals hissed in unison, charging.

Ronan met the first with brute force, driving his shoulder into the creature's chest and slamming it through a rusted steel pillar. The impact sent a spray of metal sparks into the air. The second lunged at Elias, but a burst of blue flame erupted from the ground beneath it, knocking it back.

Elias clutched his bleeding shoulder. "Told you I had something new."

Ronan smirked. "Next time, lead with that."

The second feral lunged again, but this time Isla arrived, silver blade spinning. She drove it straight through the vampire's back, piercing the heart.

The creature screeched and crumbled.

They regrouped, breath heavy, surrounded by corpses that were already beginning to disintegrate.

Camilla crouched beside Elias. "You alright?"

"I'll live. Barely."

Ronan looked at Isla. "These weren't random attacks. They were waiting for us."

"Katerina's pushing harder," Isla said, pacing. "She's testing our limits. Trying to see how fast we respond, how many we can handle."

"She wants to bleed us dry before the real fight," Elias added grimly.

Camilla stood. "Then we don't give her time."

Back at the Safehouse

Later that night, the map had more red pins. Too many. But there were patterns now, lines forming a cage around the city centre.

"She's trying to isolate us," Elias said, arm wrapped in bandages. "Divide the districts. Cut communications. Keep her ferals between the cracks."

"And she's still not showing herself," Ronan growled.

Isla looked at the pins. Then at the street names. "She's circling Castlefield again. That's where her nest was."

"She abandoned it," Camilla said. "We checked it. Nothing left."

Isla shook her head. "Maybe. Or maybe she wants us to think she ran."

She tapped the map. "There's another place. A barge tunnel under the canal. Not connected to the official records. I found it years ago."

Camilla frowned. "You thinking what I'm thinking?"

Isla nodded. "We go in. Quiet. Small team. If she's there…"

"We finish it," Ronan said.

Elias picked up his dagger. "Or die trying."

Isla's gaze burned with purpose. "No. We survive. We end this."

Outside, lightning rolled over the city as the team readied themselves, unaware that in the shadows, Katerina watched their every move.

Smiling.

Because the true threat was still to come.

Chapter 16: Into the Tunnels

The storm broke above Manchester, a sheet of rain pounding the streets with thunderous rhythm. Beneath it all, where light barely reached and the air was thick with damp stone and secrets, Isla led the team into the depths of the canal tunnels beneath Castlefield.

The entrance was tucked behind a broken iron gate, hidden under a rotting dock where forgotten boats once moored. Ronan wrenched it open with a grunt, the metal groaning in protest. The scent that greeted them was foul, mildew, mold... and something else. Something older. Staler.

Blood.

Not fresh. Not human.

Isla went first, stepping into the darkness with her blade drawn and senses on edge. Her wolf bristled beneath her skin, pacing in the back of her mind. The walls were slick with condensation, and the ceiling arched above them in tight brick vaults. Old canal water sloshed beside the footpath, black and motionless.

Camilla clicked on her flashlight. "I swear, if we find rats the size of cats down here, I'm out."

Elias gave a dry chuckle. "That's not what you need to worry about."

Ronan followed at the rear, his axe slung across his shoulder. "You can feel it, can't you?" he said quietly. "The air. The stillness."

Isla nodded. "This place has seen death. Not recently, but it's tainted."

The team moved in silence for another twenty feet before Isla suddenly raised a hand. They froze. She tilted her head, listening. Water dripping. Stone creaking. Then,

Whispers.

Soft and ragged, like breath on cold glass. Not words. Not quite. But voices nonetheless.

They moved toward it.

Around a bend, the tunnel widened into an ancient service chamber, half-flooded, with collapsed brickwork and a rusted ladder leading to a grate far above. The scent was stronger here. The corruption thick, as though the very stone was sweating blood.

Ronan moved beside Isla. "Look."

Bones. Half a dozen skeletons in varying stages of decay, piled carelessly in the far corner, some still wrapped in the tattered remains of modern clothes, hoodies, denim jackets, a pair of trainers.

"They were fed on," Elias said grimly, kneeling. "Quickly. Not cleanly."

Camilla's light caught something, scratches in the wall. At first glance, they looked like damage from tools or stone collapse. But as Isla leaned in, her breath caught.

Names.

Hundreds of them, scrawled in claw marks across the surface, like a ledger of the dead. Some were modern. Some old. Some... ancient.

One name, fresh and deep, stood out among the rest: **ISLA**.

Camilla backed up. "That's."

"She knew we'd come," Isla muttered.

A slow clap echoed from the shadows beyond.

They spun around, weapons raised.

From the darkness emerged two ferals, their eyes burning red, bodies twisted. Behind them, half-concealed in a deeper archway, a figure stepped into view.

Not Katerina.

Another vampire.

Older. Male. Refined but cruel in posture, with pale skin that looked almost translucent and veins like vines beneath it. His lips curled in a smile, but his eyes were dead things.

"You're not welcome in these halls," he said.

Isla stepped forward. "We're not here for you."

"I know. But you're trespassing in her territory." He tilted his head. "And she's not fond of interruptions."

The ferals lunged.

Ronan moved like lightning, cleaving one in half before it hit the floor. Isla rolled under the other, slashing its tendon and driving her blade through its chest. It hissed and clawed wildly, catching her across the thigh before going limp.

Camilla fired her gun, the silver rounds catching the edge of the vampire's coat, but he was already moving, disappearing back into the darkness.

"Coward," Ronan snarled.

Isla pressed her hand to her bleeding leg, grimacing. "He was a lieutenant. Not one of the ferals. More controlled."

"Which means Katerina's building more than an army of rabid monsters," Elias said, shaking his head. "She's organizing. She has structure."

Camilla knelt beside one of the fallen ferals, frowning. "What the hell are we up against?"

Isla looked again at the wall. At the names. At hers.

"She's not just feeding," she whispered. "She's keeping score."

Back at the Safehouse – Later

Maps were laid out. The photos from the tunnels pinned alongside new ones—new victims, pulled from alleys and canals over the last forty-eight hours.

"This is escalating fast," Elias said. "The ferals are bait. Distractions. The real network is moving under our noses."

"And the elder in the tunnels?" Camilla asked. "He's not part of her game?"

"No," Isla said, certain. "He didn't serve her. He warned us. In his way."

"She's playing with power beyond her control," Ronan muttered. "And we're running out of time."

Elias looked up. "We need to push back. Hard."

"Agreed," Isla said. "Let's find her next nest. And this time, we burn it down."

Chapter 17: The Fire Line

The storm had passed, but the air in Manchester still crackled with a strange electricity, like the city itself was holding its breath.

Isla stood on the rooftop of the safehouse in the early hours of morning, watching the horizon begin to burn with pale light. Below, the city stirred, oblivious to the war bleeding through its shadows.

She didn't know how long she'd been standing there when Ronan joined her.

"You're not sleeping," he said.

She didn't turn. "Neither are you."

He crossed the rooftop, the night wind tugging his coat back just enough for her to see the tension coiled in his body. "You were thinking about the names in the tunnel?"

"I'm thinking about *why* she left them."

Ronan leaned against the low stone wall beside her. "She's trying to get in your head."

"Then she's succeeding." Isla finally met his eyes. "She's been three steps ahead of us. Every time we act, she's already moved. She's leaving messages,

Ronan. She's taunting us. That doesn't feel like the Katerina we thought we were up against."

"She's changing," Ronan said. "Power does that."

"No... something's *driving* her."

Back Inside – Strategy Room

Elias had turned the dining table into a war room. Pins, maps, photos, evidence tags, each one detailing a growing trail of death. A cluster of red pushpins had started to form an ominous shape across the west side of the city.

"She's nesting near water," he muttered. "Abandoned stations. Warehouses. Sewer junctions. These aren't just hideouts, they're tactical points. Control of movement."

Camilla frowned. "Control for what?"

Elias pointed to a place just outside the city: *Ordsall Lane Depot*, long abandoned and sealed off since the '90s. "This is our best bet. It's the only site not yet hit with police interference. No cameras, no foot traffic."

Ronan circled it with a thick black marker. "It's isolated. If she's planning something bigger, this would be the staging ground."

Isla's gaze darkened. "Then that's where we go."

The Depot – Just Before Midnight

They approached from both sides, the team split into tactical pairs, Isla with Ronan, Camilla with Elias. The old depot loomed like a monolith in the dark, its massive, curved roof cracked with ivy and age.

Inside, it was vast, an open concrete hanger littered with rusting rails and derelict carriages. Light filtered in through broken panels above. But it wasn't empty.

Six ferals crouched around a feeding body, fresh kill. Two more flanked an old train engine, keeping watch.

Isla signalled silently.

Go.

Ronan launched first, his axe splitting a feral from shoulder to chest in a brutal arc. Isla followed, blades flashing with precise fury. They moved like twin storms, fluid, practiced, unrelenting.

Camilla opened fire from the left, her silver rounds scattering the ferals into disarray. Elias raised his hands and murmured something under his breath, the air shimmered, and a ripple of force exploded outward, knocking two vampires flat against the steel siding.

But then something changed.

A scream tore through the air, not from a feral, but from above.

They all looked up.

A figure descended from the rafters like a wraith. Clad in blood-red silk and dripping with menace, Katerina landed in a crouch atop the old engine. Her eyes gleamed like garnets. Her smile was sharp enough to cut glass.

"You brought the whole pack," she said, her voice smooth, amused.

Isla stepped forward. "It ends tonight."

Katerina's expression twisted with something between rage and ecstasy. "Oh, no. Tonight is just the beginning."

She raised her hand, and a symbol burned red into the engine's side, a strange glyph, ancient, pulsing with dark energy.

Elias inhaled sharply. "That's not vampire magic. That's… older."

The ground shuddered.

Something stirred beneath them.

From the shadows of the pit in the depot floor, an unnatural sound echoed, a low, rumbling growl that no human or vampire should have made.

Katerina vanished in a blur of speed.

A heartbeat later, a monstrous feral, far larger than any they'd faced before, erupted from the pit, spine protruding, teeth like obsidian daggers, and eyes glowing with pure crimson fire. It had been twisted, corrupted.

It wasn't just a feral. It was an experiment.

"Back!" Isla shouted, slicing at it as Ronan leapt in to flank. The creature shrugged off the blows like they were feathers.

Camilla threw a silver grenade, one of Elias's creations. The creature shrieked as it exploded in a burst of light, disorienting it just long enough for Ronan to land a heavy, brutal blow to its neck.

Still not enough.

"Elias, anything?" Isla yelled.

Elias was at the glyph, chanting in a language that made Isla's skin crawl. The symbol pulsed brighter, then cracked. The creature staggered. Isla took the opportunity, drove her silver blade into its chest.

The creature howled. Then, silence.

It fell.

Panting, Isla looked around the now-quiet depot. The ferals were dead. The team alive.

But the symbol on the train engine had left a charred mark, and as Elias examined it, his face paled.

"This wasn't just a test of strength," he said. "This was a summoning seal."

"Summoning what?" Camilla asked.

Isla met Elias's gaze.

He swallowed. "She's not building an army for herself. She's building it... for *someone else*."

A long pause.

"Someone older than the vampire line."

Ronan stepped forward. "You think she's trying to raise one of the Ancients."

Elias nodded grimly. "And if she succeeds, Manchester won't just fall. The whole supernatural balance collapses with it."

Isla sheathed her blade. "Then we stop her. No matter what it takes."

Chapter 18: Echoes of the Ancient

The light from Elias's torch flickered as they moved deeper into the depot's substructure, beneath the rails and broken engines, where no blueprints had ever been drawn. The ground here wasn't concrete anymore, it was packed earth, long buried and long forgotten. The smell of blood and decay lingered, thick and cloying, but beneath it… something older. Dusty. Cryptic.

Elias knelt near the shattered glyph, his fingers hovering over the scorched lines.

"This wasn't made by her," he muttered. "Not originally. This is centuries old, maybe older. She activated it, twisted it, but the seal itself? It was already here."

Ronan crossed his arms. "So, this place isn't just a hideout."

"It's a gate," Elias said softly.

Camilla glanced at Isla. "A gate to what?"

Isla didn't answer.

She didn't need to. The chill crawling down her spine said enough.

Elias stood, brushing dirt from his hands, his expression tense. "There were rumours in the old texts, fragments, half-destroyed tomes, of Deep Veins. Tunnels buried by magic and time, created in the First Era when the vampire courts still ruled from the shadows. Not all of them were destroyed after the wars. Some were sealed. Some... like this... simply forgotten."

"But forgotten by who?" Isla asked. "The vampires? The humans? The elders?"

"Everyone," Elias said grimly. "Because what was beneath them wasn't just dangerous, it was forbidden. These places weren't just prisons or nests. They were vessels. Tombs, maybe. Meant to hold power no one should ever touch again."

Ronan's voice dropped. "You think she found one."

"I think," Elias said, "she's trying to open it."

Later That Night, Safehouse War Room

They reconvened; the tension thick as the evidence piled before them. Photos from the depot. Markings on the walls. The corrupted feral's body, now locked in Elias's magical stasis chamber, twitching even in death.

Elias had already begun piecing together the symbols.

"She's not building an army to fight us. Not just us," he corrected. "She's trying to build a shield. A front line."

"Against what?" Camilla asked.

Elias looked over at Isla, then Ronan. "Against whatever lies below."

He pulled open a black-bound journal, pages brittle and worn.

"This came from the hidden archives in Wales. It references something only ever referred to as *Voro Noctis*. The Night Hunger."

Isla frowned. "That's a myth. Something used to scare fledgling wolves during full moon rites."

Elias shook his head. "It was real enough that three vampire monarchs formed a covenant with the remaining werewolf clans and fae courts to seal it away. No creature could control it. Not even their own kind. Some believed it to be an Ancient, a progenitor vampire, older than blood itself. Others thought it was a failed experiment, part god, part void, born from the chaos before the first veil was torn open."

"And now Katerina is poking the embers," Ronan said coldly. "Hoping to summon a fire she can't control."

"She thinks she can tame it," Elias replied. "Or use it. And she's willing to sacrifice the entire city to try."

The Balance, At Risk

The implications were staggering.

Isla sat back in her chair, staring at the string of photos across the wall. Bite marks, torn limbs, mutilated ferals, the glyph. The escalation wasn't random. It was methodical. Like she was testing the limits of how far she could go before the supernatural order pushed back.

"We can't just fight this in the streets," Isla said, voice low. "If she's really tapping into something from before the last war, we're looking at the collapse of everything we've built since."

"The vampire accords," Ronan added. "The treaties, the hidden alliances… the neutrality pacts."

"If the higher covens find out Katerina's breaking the Bloodbound Covenant, turning without permission, raising forbidden magic, there'll be blood. But not just hers." Elias stood. "The moment they step out of the shadows to enforce their law, humans will know. The veil will fall."

"And the second that happens," Isla murmured, "the war starts all over again."

Ronan's jaw tightened. "We lost too many last time. Wolves. Witches. Humans caught in the crossfire. That cannot happen again."

Camilla leaned forward. "So, what's the play?"

"We hunt her down," Isla said. "We shut her down. Before anyone higher up realises what she's doing. Before the ancient thing under the city gets a chance to wake up."

"But first," Elias added, "we need to know where she's gone."

Katerina's New Sanctum

The room was carved from black stone, not built but grown, older than even Katerina could explain. She walked barefoot across the glyph-etched floor, blood still drying on her hands.

She stared into the void of the summoning pool. It pulsed now. It breathed.

"Soon," she whispered.

Behind her, two freshly turned ferals shivered in the corner, still twitching with madness. One had failed, already frothing at the mouth. The other clung to sanity with fractured claws.

She didn't care. Failures were part of the climb. She only needed a few that worked.

She touched the obsidian wall. A whisper touched her mind.

A voice. Ancient. Alien. Hungry.

It said her name.

Katerina.

She smiled.

"I will be Queen. And when I open the gate, you will rise... and everything they know will burn."

Chapter 19: Crossroads

The rain hadn't let up for hours.

It fell in heavy sheets, blanketing the Manchester skyline in a grim haze of neon lights and dripping rooftops. In the heart of the city, where alleyways curved like veins and old buildings wore soot like skin, Isla stood with her back pressed to the crumbling brick of a warehouse wall.

She closed her eyes and breathed in deep.

Blood. Wet stone. Smoke. A whisper of magic on the air, faint, but pulsing.

Something was close.

Behind her, Camilla adjusted the grip on her sidearm, casting a glance down the street. Elias was halfway up a fire escape, scanning rooftops for signs of movement. Ronan remained in the shadows across the road, silent and watchful, his wolf senses drinking in the chaos.

"Tell me again why we split up?" Camilla asked under her breath.

"To cover more ground," Isla replied, "and because time is slipping."

Katerina hadn't made another public move since the attack at the industrial estate. But the silence wasn't reassuring, it was ominous. A tactical pause. A breath before the purge.

Elias descended, jumping the last few rungs and landing lightly beside them.

"Nothing on the rooftops. But the energy here... it's different. Like something passed through hours ago, maybe less."

He pointed toward the narrow alley ahead.

"There's residual trail magic. Not hers directly, but someone connected to her. A scout, maybe."

Isla gave a curt nod. "Then we track it."

The Whisper Beneath the Church

Ronan didn't tell the others where he was going.

He'd peeled away from the group under the guise of checking another lead near Deansgate, but instead he'd driven out past the ring road, weaving through streets few humans dared tread after dark. His destination: St. Ethelred's, a long-condemned church on the edge of Angel Meadow, where the air always felt colder and the shadows moved too easily.

He knew who dwelled beneath it.

A contact. An ancient one.

Not a friend, but not an enemy either.

"Debt repaid," the message had said. *"You'll find answers in the hollow beneath the broken bells."*

He left his car two streets over and made the final approach on foot. The doors to the church hung crooked, but he didn't enter through the front. Instead, Ronan dropped down a side stairwell behind the overgrown cemetery, into the catacombs that threaded beneath the old building like veins.

There, among the collapsed tombs and moss-slick walls, waited *Morven*.

She was fae, but not the polished, glamoured sort that slipped through high society. Morven was one of the Old Blood, changeless since before Roman walls rose around Manchester. Her skin had the pallor of moonlight, dappled with cracks like marble. Her eyes glowed violet in the dark.

"Alpha." She never used his name. "You look older."

"You look like death," Ronan growled in return.

Morven smiled, showing blackened teeth. "You came for whispers."

Ronan tossed a folded cloth into her lap, a charm stitched in iron and red thread. "Payment."

She sniffed it delicately. "Fair enough. What do you want to know?"

"Katerina. What is she doing? What's she looking for beneath the city?"

Morven traced a claw across the cracked stone at her feet, then gestured to the sigils drawn around them in ash and salt.

"She asked about the *Vein*. The true one. You think the leylines that spider beneath Manchester are just raw power, don't you? Old tunnels filled with sleeping energy. But the Vein, *the* Vein, is more than that. It's a tether. A spine connecting what was to what will be."

Ronan crouched, frowning. "Tethered to what?"

"To the Wound," she whispered. "A rift carved during the vampire wars, when a being older than the clans tore through this realm and was barely held back. That gate wasn't destroyed. Just buried. Forgotten. Sealed by pact and pain and blood."

Ronan's stomach turned cold. "And Katerina is trying to find it?"

"She doesn't know what it is," Morven said, suddenly still. "Not fully. But she knows it's old, and she knows it thrums with power."

She turned her gaze to him, eyes sharp now, focused.

"She's calling out through it, Alpha. And something is listening. Something that remembers being trapped. The gate stirs. And if she breaks the seals."

"She won't," Ronan cut in, standing abruptly. "She won't get that far."

Morven tilted her head.

"Then you'd better run faster, wolf. Because the Vein remembers your kind too. It remembers your war cries. Your blood. And if it wakes… it will hunger for vengeance."

Ronan crouched in the basement of the once-abandoned church, now the quiet sanctum of the underground fae merchant. The old being blinked slowly, luminous eyes reflecting the dim glow of the sigils placed across the floor.

"You were right to come. But wrong to hope you're in time."

Ronan's eyes narrowed. "Why?"

"Because the gate no longer sleeps. It *listens* now."

The old fae tapped a bony finger on the floor, and the sigils flared in brief, violent red.

"She calls to it, and it calls back. And it remembers."

Regrouping at the Safehouse

Isla slammed the heavy door shut behind her, shrugging off her soaked coat.

They all looked worn, exhausted from the chase. Elias rubbed his temples. Camilla dried her gun with a tea towel, muttering something about "normal crime scenes" and "bloody monsters."

"Did we get anything concrete?" Isla asked.

Elias dropped a bloodstained cloth onto the table. "Found this at a warehouse near Salford Quays. Not Katerina's blood, but someone recently turned. They're nesting in abandoned sites all over now, small pockets. Spread out. Controlled."

"They're preparing for something," Camilla added. "They're not feeding wildly anymore. It's almost… calculated."

Ronan nodded, his expression grim. "I heard the same. She's creating cells, dividing her forces. Classic war strategy. You strike from different angles. Test weak points. Distract."

"And while we chase her soldiers…" Isla said quietly, "she digs deeper into the Veins."

There was silence then.

A weight settled across the room, heavy with understanding.

"She's not just building an army," Elias said slowly. "She's mapping the old ley line network beneath the city. If she can anchor her power into those places."

"She could spread her influence across the entire urban sprawl," Isla finished. "And if she opens the wrong gate…"

"She won't control what comes through."

Isla stared at the map Elias had unfurled across the table, veins of ley lines and underground structures scrawled between half-drunk mugs of tea and bloodied gauze.

The pieces weren't falling into place, they were crashing together. This wasn't just a rogue vampire building a nest. Katerina was reaching for something buried in vampire history, something tied to the old wars, the same wars that nearly annihilated their kind.

Whatever she'd found, whatever pulsed beneath the city, wasn't a god or some otherworldly beast clawing through the veil. It was vampire-made. Vampire-bound. A relic of blood and power left behind when the clans fell, sealed away for a reason. And now...

Katerina wanted to wake it.

Beneath the City

Katerina paced slowly around the blood-washed circle, her bare feet leaving no print. The four vampires kneeling before her did not move. One twitched. One sobbed quietly. The others simply stared, slack-jawed and glassy-eyed.

Above them, a map of Manchester had been etched into the stone, glowing faintly with enchanted light.

"We are ready for the next phase," she said softly, almost lovingly. "Each of you will take a quadrant. You'll begin the sowing."

Her nails dug into one of their shoulders. The vampire gasped.

"If you fail... you'll beg for death before I grant it."

The blood glyphs along the walls pulsed. The gate pulsed with them.

And the *thing* beyond it whispered its pleasure.

Back at the Safehouse, Midnight Plans

"We need to hit her next site before she makes her next move," Isla said, pointing to a section of the city where the ley lines crossed beneath an old Victorian train station.

"Old Trafford," Elias muttered. "Christ. She's headed for one of the most magically volatile junctures in the north."

Ronan stepped forward, cracking his knuckles.

"Then we'll be there first."

Chapter 20: Echoes Beneath the Stone

The catacombs beneath Manchester's city centre weren't listed on any official map. Forgotten passageways buried beneath centuries of construction, used once for war shelters, then by smugglers, and finally swallowed whole by time and silence. But Elias had found them, traced through old fae texts and warded books he shouldn't have had access to. And now the team stood at the rusting service entrance beneath an abandoned train station, the air thick with mildew, iron, and something darker.

Camilla clicked on her torch. "Smells like a tomb."

"It *is* a tomb," Elias replied grimly, pulling a sigil-laced flare from his coat. "Just not the kind they ever meant the living to return from."

They descended in near silence, Isla leading with her senses wide open, the burn of blood on stone and the scratch of power old enough to taste. Ronan flanked her, his energy taut and wild beneath the surface, eyes shifting gold in the low light.

"There's movement," Isla said lowly, her voice a breath more than a sound. "Ahead. And behind."

"They know we're here," Ronan muttered. "Let's hope they're not the talkative type."

The tunnel opened into a wide vault-like chamber carved in layers of stone and bone, remnants of ancient vampire script etched into every surface. In the centre stood a dais, and what looked like the remnants of a ritual circle long dried of blood. The flare in Elias's hand pulsed softly as they stepped inside.

"This is where she did it," he said. "Turned them. Fed them something old. Not just blood… Something else. Something buried in the vampire gene itself."

Camilla crouched near the edge of the circle, running her gloved fingers through a sticky residue that hadn't fully dried. "This isn't fresh. She's been here more than once."

Suddenly, a hiss cut through the silence. Shadows peeled from the walls like smoke made solid.

"Eyes!" Ronan growled, shifting mid-step into his wolf form, silver fur bristling with fury. Isla followed a half-second later, her transformation smooth, practiced, deadly.

The ferals dropped from the shadows, more agile than the last ones, eyes gleaming red, movements erratic and fast. Whatever Katerina had fed them, it made them faster. Meaner.

The fight exploded.

Elias flung runes across the floor that detonated in arcs of silver fire. Ronan tore through one feral, jaws snapping its neck with brutal precision. Isla danced between two others, claws slashing, her mind calm even as adrenaline surged.

But they just kept coming.

"Back-to-back!" she barked, blood flying as she spun and raked through another attacker. "Camilla, the flare!"

Camilla struck the trigger. The circle flared to life with a pulse of light, revealing glyphs that hadn't been visible before, vampire markings, yes, but mixed with fae language and something even older.

"Elias!" Isla shouted, dragging a feral down with her as it tried to get behind him. "What the hell does it say?"

He squinted, bleeding from a cut above his eye. "It's a binding script. Katerina's trying to unlock something, not from another realm, but buried beneath the old vampire clans. Bloodline magic. She's resurrecting a forgotten blood court!"

Isla froze for half a beat. A court. A lineage.

So this wasn't just about territory.

This was about *thrones*.

The last feral shrieked and collapsed as Ronan drove his claws through its chest, panting hard as the echoes of the fight faded. Camilla leaned against a wall, bruised but intact, torchlight flickering over her face.

"So… she's trying to bring back ancient vampire royalty?" she asked, voice strained.

"Or become one herself," Elias replied, standing in the now-glowing circle. "Either way, we're already out of time."

Isla looked down at the old symbols, at the blood etched into stone, and knew, the next move Katerina made would tip the balance. Whatever court she was invoking had been sealed away by those who understood what power meant… and what it could destroy.

And now it was waking up.

Chapter 21: The Call to Shadows

The storm broke as they emerged from the tunnels. Rain lashed the city streets like knives from the sky, washing the blood and grime from Isla's skin but not the tension from her bones. Camilla limped slightly, an angry gash taped up tight. Ronan remained in his wolf form longer than usual, eyes scanning every shadow until they reached the safehouse.

Elias was already inside, pouring over a spread of books and scrolls, his hands shaking as he laid the symbols they'd seen in the tunnels side by side with ancient clan sigils.

"Anything?" Isla asked, dragging a chair closer.

Elias looked up, dark rings under his eyes. "No one's summoned blood court symbols in over a thousand years. Most thought the last of that line was wiped out in the Great War. If Katerina's tapping into them... she's not just ambitious. She's suicidal. And she's going to take the rest of us down with her."

Isla slammed her fist on the table, the sound sharp. "Then why hasn't the hierarchy stopped her? Where the hell *are* they?"

That silence said everything.

"They're watching," Ronan growled, now fully shifted back, eyes still glowing faintly. "Like they always do. Waiting to see who survives, who they can still control."

"They'll do nothing until the damage is irreversible," Elias said quietly. "It's always been that way. That's how the old clans survived, neutrality and denial."

"Then we rip the veil down," Camilla said, surprising everyone with the venom in her voice. "You all keep saying how delicate the balance is, how fragile things are between humans and the supernatural. But if Katerina gets what she wants, there won't *be* any balance left."

Isla stood, fire burning in her chest. "Then we call them out. I don't care about their rules or their silence. I'll drag their secrets into the daylight if I have to."

Ronan nodded, jaw set. "We'll need more than a name. We'll need a summons. One that *forces* them to listen."

Elias hesitated, then reached beneath the desk and pulled out a shard of obsidian bound in gold wire. "This is vampire court law. Very old. Dangerous. You use it, and they'll come. But you don't get to choose how they answer."

"Good," Isla said. "Because I'm done waiting."

They chose the location carefully, an abandoned theatre beneath Manchester's Northern Quarter, long-since sealed from the public, warded and steeped in old power. Ronan etched the sigils across the walls while Elias lit the perimeter with bone-white candles. Camilla stood watch near the entrance, double-checking every escape route.

When the obsidian shard cracked in Isla's palm, the air turned cold. Not the chill of winter, but the ancient cold of breath held too long, of bones sealed in stone.

And then… they came.

Figures stepped from the shadows, not through doors, but *through* the veil itself. A man in a dark coat whose skin shimmered like oil on water. A woman in silver who moved like a dancer, though her eyes held centuries of violence. Another, taller, featureless, as though wrapped in smoke.

They said nothing.

"You know who I am," Isla began. "I'm not a member of your court. I'm not part of your games. But what Katerina is doing, what you're *letting* her do, isn't just reckless. It's treasonous. She's risking exposure, war, and the deaths of thousands. Supernatural and human alike."

The one wrapped in smoke tilted its head. "She acts outside our sanction."

"But she still bears your mark," Ronan growled. "And your silence makes you complicit."

The woman finally stepped forward. Her voice was silk layered in steel. "She seeks power she does not understand. She invokes bloodlines sealed by pact and by curse. We are aware. But interference carries… weight."

"Then maybe you need a reminder of what's at stake," Camilla said, stepping forward. "Bodies are piling up in the streets. And not all of them are staying dead."

The man in the dark coat spoke, his voice like stone cracking. "You are not part of our court. You speak with borrowed power, borrowed blood."

"No," Isla said coldly. "I speak as someone trying to *stop a war*. And if you won't stop her, I *will*. But don't think I'll keep your secrets when the city burns."

That landed. The room seemed to tense, even the air holding its breath.

"Then know this," the woman said. "If you move against Katerina… you move alone."

Isla's jaw clenched. "So be it."

The figures dissolved into shadow one by one, leaving only silence and the crackle of dying flame behind.

As the last echo vanished, Ronan stepped beside her.

"We're really doing this without them."

"We always were."

Chapter 22: Lines in the Ash

The city was holding its breath.

Above ground, traffic hummed, pubs spilled over with laughter, and the heartbeat of Manchester thrummed on like it always had. But beneath it, below the cobbles, behind closed doors, under the skin of things, something ancient was fracturing.

Isla stood in the centre of the safehouse, the scent of smoke and blood still clinging to her clothes. Her shoulders were stiff, eyes distant. Around her, the team was finally still, Ronan nursing a gash on his shoulder, Camilla scribbling down names, notes, theories on the whiteboard they'd dragged into the living room, and Elias pouring through a stack of old texts that looked like they'd been stolen from a monastery.

They had tracked, fought, and barely survived the ferals at Castlefield. But what they'd found there hadn't been a nest. It had been a warning. A taste of the scale they were facing.

"She's not hiding anymore," Isla said, voice low.

Camilla looked up from her notes. "You think she's pushing toward open war?"

"No." Isla met her gaze. "She already started it."

Ronan exhaled sharply and tossed the bloodstained towel onto the table. "I've seen rogue nests before. Desperate ones. Starving ones. But what she's doing? It's orchestrated. And these ferals… they aren't failures. They're pawns."

Elias looked up. "Created to cause chaos, to draw attention. Keep us running in circles while she consolidates power elsewhere."

Camilla's brow furrowed. "But what's the endgame? What does she *want*?"

Isla's jaw clenched. "She wants the city. She wants power. And she wants to tear down the order that's kept her kind in check for centuries."

"She's challenging the Elders," Ronan said, expression dark. "And they're doing nothing."

"Worse," Elias added. "They're *letting* it happen. Either out of fear… or arrogance."

"We gave them a chance to act," Isla said, voice quiet. "We went to the oldest of them, and they hid behind traditions. Politics. Neutrality. But this isn't about balance anymore. It's about survival."

Camilla crossed her arms. "Then what's the plan? We can't take on the vampire hierarchy and Katerina's turned army in the same breath."

"No," Isla agreed. "But we can force their hand."

Everyone stilled.

The mood inside the safehouse was brittle. Everyone had felt it, the moment the last sliver of hope they had in the vampire court had been crushed beneath centuries-old arrogance.

Ronan paced the length of the room, hands balled into fists. "They didn't even listen. Didn't look at the reports. The photos. The patterns."

"They don't care," Elias said, rubbing his temple. "To them, Katerina's a splinter. An irritation. Not a threat. They're too blind to see that she's not just breaking rules, she's trying to rewrite them."

Isla stood by the window, the rain sliding down the pane like tears she refused to let fall. "They made it clear: if we go after her, we're on our own."

Camilla, leaning back against the table, let out a low breath. "So… what? We just roll over and let her win?"

"No." Isla turned, voice like steel. "We do what we've always done. We fight."

Ronan stopped pacing. "Without backup? Without numbers?"

Elias raised a brow. "That hasn't stopped us before."

"No," Isla said. "But we can't pretend this is just about her anymore. Katerina's not trying to rule a nest. She's trying to burn down the entire system. And she's not doing it alone."

Elias looked up sharply. "You think she has help?"

"She's using rites," Isla said, pacing now herself. "Blood spells. Magic older than vampire law. She's not summoning from beyond the Veil, but she's *channelling* something, something they buried after the last war."

Ronan's gaze darkened. "Old magic."

"She's found a way to tie it into her turning. She's not just making ferals... she's testing limits. Looking for a way to create something stronger, something that obeys *her* and nothing else."

Camilla paled. "So, she's building her own kind of vampire. One outside the law. Outside tradition."

"Exactly," Isla said. "She's not playing queen. She's trying to become a god."

Silence fell. The kind that echoed through bone.

Ronan broke it. "Then we stop her before she finishes whatever she's started."

"Without the court?" Camilla asked.

Elias gave a small, crooked smile. "If they won't enforce their own laws, maybe it's time someone else did."

Isla met their eyes. "We need to hit back. But not just with brute force. We need intel. Leverage. We need to know what she's really building, and where she's hiding it."

Camilla narrowed her eyes. "Where do we start?"

Isla turned toward the whiteboard, where maps and notes and photographs overlapped in a web of chaos. She picked up a marker and circled three sites, all old, all forgotten: the old catacombs beneath Castlefield, the sealed tunnels near Mayfield Depot, and the ruins of the church that burned down on the outskirts of Ancoats nearly fifty years ago.

"Vampires store secrets in places no one wants to remember," she said. "If she's feeding her plans with blood magic, there'll be traces. Runes. Sigils. Energy."

Ronan nodded. "And if we can find them."

"We can find her," Isla finished.

Elias stood. "We'll need gear. Wards. And stealth. If she gets wind of this."

"She won't," Isla said. "Because we won't come through the front."

Camilla arched a brow. "And if we do find something? Something big?"

Isla looked out the window again. Rain. Thunder in the distance. The city unaware of the storm brewing beneath its streets.

"Then we burn her world to the ground before she burns ours."

Chapter 23: Of Silver Tongues and Old Magic

The fire in the hearth crackled, low and steady. Outside, the city roared, sirens in the distance, wind lashing at windows, but inside the safehouse, the air was dense. Heavy with decisions unspoken.

Isla sat at the edge of the dining table, her leg bouncing. She could feel something rising, a change in the current. Whether it was from Katerina's hand or something deeper, she couldn't yet tell.

Ronan stood with his arms folded near the window, watching the storm. He hadn't spoken in nearly ten minutes. Not since Isla had marked the three ritual sites on the board.

It was Elias who finally broke the silence. "You've been quiet too long. That usually means you're about to say something reckless."

Ronan didn't flinch. "I've been thinking."

"That's always worrying," Camilla muttered under her breath.

He turned slowly, his gaze flicking over the group. "Before I found Isla in the tunnels that day, I was following a thread of something else. A presence. Something not vampire."

Isla looked up sharply. "You said you just picked up the trail."

"I lied," Ronan said simply. "Because I didn't know what I was dealing with. I followed a shimmer, a pull in the air, a hunch, ended up paying someone of old a visit out at St Ethelreds."

Isla blinked. "No one goes out there anymore."

"Not unless something calls them," Ronan agreed. "And something did."

Elias leaned forward. "What did you see?"

"A Woman," Ronan said. "A Fae, Pale. Voice like steel and water. Said he wasn't allowed to interfere, but she could… tip the scales. Said Katerina was stirring old echoes. Bloodlines older than vampires. Older than wolves."

Camilla snorted. "Okay. Time out. Are you all just making this shit up as we go? Vampires, werewolves, now Fae? What's next, dragons?"

Ronan smirked. "You wanted the truth, Detective. And dragon shifters do exist, they're just very few and far between"

"I wanted answers," Camilla said, pointing a finger. "Not an episode of Mythical Madness: Northern Edition."

Elias chuckled. "Actually, Fae aren't a myth. Not in our world. They're just elusive. Their magic is... different. Slippery. Bound by rules older than language. Most of them don't care about human affairs unless something *big* is at stake."

"And they spoke to you?" Isla asked, ignoring Camilla's half-smile.

Ronan nodded. "Didn't give a name. Just said the balance was tipping too far. That if the vampires didn't correct the course, someone else would. That 'the bloodbound would have to act before the covenant burned.'"

Elias stilled. "Bloodbound. She used that word?"

"Yes."

Elias got up abruptly and started rifling through the books on the side shelf. Old tomes, half in Latin, some in ink that shimmered silver under the light. He pulled one free, *Magia Obscura: Threads of the Forgotten Realms*, and flipped quickly through the pages.

Camilla arched a brow. "You just happen to have Fae books lying around?"

Elias didn't look up. "I happen to have everything lying around."

"Comforting."

He stopped on a page marked with what looked like an old sigil, a half-moon tangled in thorns. "Here. The Bloodbound Covenant. It was a pact. A ceasefire forged between Fae and Vampire kind after the last war. Before the Veil was sealed."

Isla moved to his side, eyes narrowing on the text. "So, if the Fae are stirring now…"

"It means something's violating that ancient pact," Elias finished. "And if Katerina's doing magic that presses on their side of the boundary…"

"They'll push back," Ronan said. "Hard."

Camilla rubbed her face. "So let me get this straight, not only do we have to deal with a psychotic vampire trying to start her own kingdom, but now there's the magical version of Interpol watching us from the woods?"

"Not watching," Elias said. "Waiting. For us to fail."

"Great."

Isla folded her arms. "Can we use this? The Fae magic?"

Elias hesitated. "Fae magic isn't cast. It's… negotiated. Traded. It always comes with a price. But if we can find the right path, the right artifact or pact fragment."

"It might give us the edge we need," Ronan said.

Isla nodded, slowly. "Then we find it. Whatever it takes."

Because Katerina was building an army.

But the Bloodbound were awakening something older.

And the city of Manchester might just become the first battleground in a war no one remembered how to survive.

Chapter 24: Fractures in the Pact

The cold morning sun barely pierced the clouded sky as Manchester stirred to life, unaware of the war brewing beneath its streets. Somewhere in the heart of the city, a vampire queen was plotting her next move. And across the city, a fractured alliance of wolves, scholars, and mortals raced to uncover the secrets that could stop her.

Isla stood in the quiet courtyard behind Elias' townhouse, breathing in the frosted air. The ache in her ribs from the last fight had dulled to a distant throb, but tension coiled tighter with every passing hour.

Inside, the others made preparations, gear being packed, information traded, plans drawn. They were splitting up today. Too many threats, too few leads. And time… time was slipping.

Elias joined her, a small satchel of books and notes slung across his shoulder. "There's a record of a place," he said softly. "Just outside the Peak District. A burial site. Not human, not quite Fae either, something in between. The last time the Covenant was mentioned in any physical text, it was in connection to that location."

Isla tilted her head. "And you think something's buried there?"

"I think if we want a chance at finding a way to stop Katerina, we need to understand what deal she's violating, and what the other side might do to stop her."

She nodded once. "You'll go?"

"With Camilla," Elias confirmed. "She insisted. Said if I got myself hexed by a fairy ghost, someone had to drag me out."

Isla smirked. "Sounds like her."

Elias glanced toward the townhouse. "And you?"

"I'm going with Ronan," she said, voice sharpening. "There's a contact in the old wolf networks. Someone who may have information on vampire movements in the city from before Katerina showed up. If anyone noticed a change in patterns, it'll be him."

Elias' brow furrowed. "Do you trust him?"

"Enough."

A beat passed.

"Ronan said something, before you came down," Elias said. "He thinks Katerina's next move is bigger than just building an army. He thinks she's trying to trigger the Fae into crossing the line."

"On purpose?"

Elias nodded grimly. "He thinks she *wants* a war. With the humans as the battlefield."

Isla's stomach twisted. The Veil had held for centuries, an unspoken boundary between the hidden supernatural and the sleeping mortal world. If that barrier fell…

She turned sharply toward the door. "Then we stop her before she lights the fuse."

Later that Day – Outside the City Limits

The air grew colder as Ronan's truck rolled down a winding path flanked by skeletal trees, far from the last breath of city lights. Snow clung in the hollows of the land, unbothered by tire tracks or time. This was old ground, untouched, and for good reason.

Isla sat in silence, watching frost etch webs along the window. There was something *off* about this place. Not threatening exactly, but strange in a way that scraped at her wolf instincts. The energy shifted subtly with each passing mile.

Ronan finally slowed, pulling into a wide clearing nestled between stone crags. In its centre, half-sunken into the earth, stood a weathered stone circle, ancient and cracked, but humming with latent power. Moss and ice climbed its edges like fingers, and the air shimmered faintly, like heat haze in reverse.

"He won't meet us anywhere else," Ronan muttered, cutting the engine. "Says the blood sings louder out here."

Isla arched a brow. "That a metaphor or a warning?"

"With him, it's usually both."

She followed him out into the stillness. The moment her boots hit the earth, something tugged at her. not her wolf, but something older. A whisper. A weight. She tensed.

A shadow separated from the treeline with impossible smoothness.

He appeared tall and lean, dressed in simple, weather-worn robes, layers of charcoal and deep green that moved like mist. His long hair was the colour of copper under moonlight, braided with black thorns and a single feather. Around one wrist he wore a band of woven silver, carved with symbols Isla didn't recognize.

His eyes were the thing that marked him, though, no whites, only silver irises swirling in obsidian pools, ancient and unreadable.

"Wolves," he greeted, voice soft but sharp as winter wind. "And the half-blood Alpha himself."

"Lirien," Ronan returned curtly. "Thanks for coming."

"I didn't come," Lirien said smoothly. "You stepped into *my* ground."

Isla stiffened, arms folded. "So, this is your territory?"

"Not territory," Lirien replied, tilting his head toward her. "Refuge."

He walked in slow circles around the stone ring, fingers brushing the old carvings as he moved. "The Court cast me out long ago. Said I cared too much for the humans. That I got... *too close*." He glanced at Isla again, smile faint. "I suppose you could say I have a weakness for creatures that live in two worlds."

"You're Fae," she said, scenting him fully now. "But... you don't smell like them."

"No," Lirien said. "Not anymore. They severed that bond. Stripped my name from the Wild Hunt's memory, unwound my blood from the ancestral lines. I live outside their Veil now. Neither court nor kind."

Ronan shifted beside her. "He chose to stay behind, when the others left centuries ago. Said someone had to keep watch. That something was *coming back*."

"Maybe I was wrong," Lirien murmured. "Or maybe I was just early."

Isla watched him carefully. There was a loneliness in him that echoed deep, a shadow of someone who'd outlived everything but regret. But there was steel beneath the sorrow.

"We need information," she said. "On Katerina. On the Covenant."

Lirien's gaze flicked to her, and for a heartbeat, the air between them thickened.

"You chase the vampire queen," he said softly. "But you are chasing her shadow. She does not fear death. She fears irrelevance. That her name will be forgotten, lost beneath the stones of time. So she carves it in blood and binds others to her will."

"She's turning humans, too many," Ronan added. "Feral. Broken. They don't last."

"She wants an army," Isla said. "But not just of vampires. She wants chaos. Power. We think she's trying to break the Covenant, push the Veil too far."

Lirien's eyes narrowed. "She already has. She's tampered with things buried for good reason. Spoke names that have not echoed since the Old Wars."

Isla's chest tightened. "Then help us stop her."

The Fae moved slowly to the centre of the stone ring, kneeling to press a palm to the frozen earth.

"There is a place," he said. "Beneath the mountains. Older than the vampire courts, older even than the first pact between wolf and moon. You will find the *Crown of Ash* there. It was once worn by the one who first crossed the Veil from my world into yours."

"What is it?" Isla asked. "A weapon?"

Lirien's voice dropped. "A key. Or a warning. Depending on who wields it."

He stood, brushing frost from his sleeve.

"You'll find it buried in the hollow beneath *Dunn's Fold*, where the sun hasn't touched the earth in centuries. But be warned, not all relics wish to be uncovered. And not all who seek power understand the price of wielding it."

Ronan looked at Isla. "Then we get there first."

"And if Katerina already knows where it is?" she asked.

Lirien's eyes turned distant. "Then you must pray you know how to stop her before she puts it on."

Meanwhile – Peak District Ruins

Camilla stood at the edge of the dig site, arms folded against the biting wind. "So," she said dryly, "we're digging up a magical burial mound under some ancient ruin of a church, in the middle of nowhere... on the word of a guy who's never seen a Fae in real life."

Elias looked up from the map. "Your sarcasm is noted."

"I'm just saying. If we get eaten by tree spirits, I'm haunting you."

"Fair."

They moved down into the exposed structure, flashlights flickering along jagged stones and moss-covered carvings. As Elias turned the corner, he froze.

There, etched deep into the wall, was the same symbol from the book, a half-moon caught in thorns.

"Found it," he whispered. "This is it."

"What does it mean?"

"That the Bloodbound Covenant is real," Elias breathed. "And Katerina's breaking something far more sacred than even the vampire court understands."

Camilla stepped back slowly. "Then we'd better stop her. Before someone, or *something*, else does it for us."

The tunnels beneath the ruined chapel twisted like veins beneath the skin of the land, old, damp, and pulsing with something that felt wrong. Camilla's boots crunched over ancient stones slick with moss and rot, her flashlight flickering as if fighting against a presence it couldn't see. Elias followed close behind, one hand skimming the cold, damp walls, murmuring faint protective charms under his breath.

"This place shouldn't exist," he muttered. "Not anymore."

Camilla arched a brow, her grip tightening on the torch. "Then why does it?"

Elias didn't answer right away. They'd already uncovered a collapsed altar upstairs carved with symbols that hadn't been used since before the last vampire war, long before their ancestors were born, long before anyone had started taking this world seriously. Down here, though, things felt... older.

Wrong.

The tunnels had led them deeper than either of them expected. What began as a simple crypt had turned into a branching maze, some passages blocked by cave-ins and roots, others branching into chambers filled with strange etchings and shattered remnants of ancient rituals.

But it was the central chamber they stood in now that made the air seem heavier.

This wasn't just a tomb.

It was a meeting place.

A long-forgotten sanctum.

The chamber was circular, the walls reinforced with blackened stone and metal braces inscribed with glyphs that pulsed faintly with a reddish hue. Scattered along the outer wall were alcoves, some of them containing shattered remnants of urns, weapons, others, rotted leather bindings still strapped to rusted chains.

Camilla crouched beside one of the alcoves and picked up a fragment of broken obsidian shaped like a fang.

"Tell me this wasn't used as some kind of sacrifice chamber."

Elias took the piece from her gently. "Not a sacrifice chamber." He knelt in the centre of the room, brushing away layers of dust and grime from a large carved emblem inlaid into the floor. "A judgment chamber."

The symbol was the same one they'd seen on the bodies in Manchester, the same sigil burned into the neck of one of the ferals: a serpent swallowing the sun, encircled in runes no vampire court should have access to.

"What is that?" Camilla asked.

"The mark of the Covenant," Elias replied, voice grim. "Not the one we know. Not the vampire treaties. *The original Covenant.*"

Camilla blinked. "You mean... older than the court?"

Elias looked up at her, his face pale. "Older than the Court. Older than the Veil as we know it."

He pointed to the serpent. "It's a warning, Camilla. This symbol was used only once in vampire history, when they first drew blood from *across the realms*. It signifies a broken pact. A war that nearly destroyed everything. The last time this symbol was seen… thousands died."

Camilla stood, arms folded. "You're telling me Katerina knows about this?"

"I'm saying she's not just building an army. She's awakening something we buried on purpose."

Behind them, the torchlight flickered again. A low hum echoed down one of the side tunnels, distant, almost like chanting.

They both turned.

"No way," Camilla whispered.

Elias drew a small iron charm from his coat pocket and flicked it toward the tunnel. It sparked in mid-air, casting a ripple of light along the stone. The glyphs hidden in the tunnel walls flared briefly, revealing a new set of carvings they hadn't seen, ones not just etched in stone but infused with blood.

"She's been here," Elias said. "Recently."

"Doing what?"

"Claiming this place. Drawing on its memory. On its power."

Camilla exhaled slowly. "So this wasn't just a sanctuary. This was…"

"A site of awakening," Elias finished. "And if she completes the ritual, she might not need the courts. She might not even need her army."

They both turned to leave, urgency pulling them faster through the tunnels.

Camilla muttered as they ascended back toward the night, "We need to burn this place to the ground."

Elias shook his head. "We need Isla."

Dunn's Fold

The moorland stretched out before them like a vast sea of frostbitten heather, the late afternoon sun casting long shadows across the broken landscape. A chill wind swept through the air, biting at Isla's neck as she zipped her jacket higher and adjusted the strap of her pack. Ronan walked beside her, his pace brisk but steady, eyes scanning the horizon as if he expected something to emerge from the mist creeping in from the peaks.

"Last time I came this way," he murmured, "the land itself tried to keep us out."

Isla glanced sideways. "That supposed to reassure me?"

Ronan smirked, but it didn't reach his eyes. "If we're lucky, the Fold won't even remember us."

They moved in silence for a while, boots crunching on brittle grass and hidden frost. The Fold wasn't a place marked on maps. It existed in the spaces between, one of those supernatural anomalies where reality blurred and the Veil ran thin. In ancient times, it was said to be a place of trial and transformation, where only those deemed worthy could pass and return with the knowledge or artifact they sought.

And now, it was where the *Crown of Ash* was hidden.

A relic of the old wars.

A weapon bound in myth.

According to Lirien, the Crown wasn't just a symbol it had been created by both vampire and wolf blood in the final hours of the last Great War, forged by an ancient faction desperate to end the bloodshed. It was meant to unite their strengths… or destroy them both if balance failed.

"Do you think it's still intact?" Isla asked, stepping carefully over a narrow stream that cut through the terrain like a silver vein.

"I think if it is, it's not going to let us near it without a fight."

They crested a rise, and there it was.

Dunn's Fold.

A hollow basin carved into the land like the scar of something ancient, unnatural. Stone pillars, weathered by time and wind, ringed the perimeter, some cracked and leaning, others glowing faintly under the mist's embrace. The air was colder here. Still. As if even the wind held its breath.

Ronan stepped into the outer ring first, his boots hitting stone with a muted thud.

"Wait," Isla said.

He turned, brows furrowed.

"I feel it," she said quietly, letting her wolf senses flood to the surface. "It's *watching* us."

"Then we're in the right place."

They moved together, eyes alert, every instinct coiled. The Fold shifted around them, the mists thickening behind their steps like a trap snapping shut. Time felt different here, slow and syrup-thick, and the ground beneath them pulsed faintly as if with memory.

As they neared the centre, the mist parted to reveal a dais made of obsidian stone, carved in the same strange script they had found with the bodies of the ferals. Resting in the centre, wrapped in thick, rust-coloured cloth, was the Crown.

And it was humming.

Low. Dangerous. Like a heart just beginning to stir after a long sleep.

Isla reached out, fingers brushing the cloth, and the world *shifted*.

She was elsewhere, not in the Fold, not in her body, but watching the past.

Flashes of war.

Wolves and vampires falling together.

A king in shadow, wearing the Crown and commanding beasts with red eyes and fire on their tongues.

And then a woman, cloaked in black, her eyes like coals, tearing the Crown from his head and casting it into the Fold, blood weeping from her palms.

Isla gasped and staggered back into her body. Ronan caught her.

"What happened?" he said.

She stilled in his arms, breathing hard. "It's not just a relic. It remembers. And it's dangerous."

Ronan knelt beside the dais and began cutting through the warding threads, careful and deliberate. "We're going to need it."

"What if we can't control it?"

"We'll find a way. Because if Katerina's reaching for the same power…" He met her gaze. "Then we can't afford to be weaker."

Suddenly, the ground trembled, faint but unmistakable. Isla spun, her eyes flashing gold.

Shapes moved in the mist, guardians of the Fold, formed of earth, bone, and magic. Their eyes glowed with molten light. Trial-wrought beasts, forged to protect the Crown.

"Looks like we woke them up," Ronan growled, eyes shifting.

Isla grinned, teeth sharp. "Good. I needed a warm-up."

Trial of the Fold

The ground shook, the stones of Dunn's Fold shivering as the guardians emerged fully from the mist, five in total. They towered, eight feet tall, each forged from stone and root, bound by ancient runes and smouldering with the slow burn of old magic. Their eyes burned molten gold, hollow and endless, and their limbs crackled as they moved.

One raised its arm, a club of fused rock and iron, and swung.

Ronan yanked Isla back just in time as the blow slammed into the ground where she'd stood, shattering stone and throwing dust skyward.

"Diplomacy's off the table?" she gasped, shifting her stance.

"Looks like trial by combat," Ronan muttered, already mid-shift, his wolf form erupting from his skin with a flash of silver fur and glowing blue eyes. He lunged, teeth flashing as he slammed into the nearest guardian.

Isla didn't shift, not yet. Instead, she tapped into the wolf beneath her skin, letting its strength roll through her limbs. Faster. Stronger. Sharper. She ducked under a guardian's swing, landed a solid kick that cracked its knee, then twisted and drew her silver-bladed dagger from her boot.

They fought like hell.

Ronan took two at once, ducking and weaving with the fluid strength of an Alpha, his claws raking across enchanted stone, buying space and time. Isla danced between the others, her strikes precise, her movements honed by years of surviving outside the pack. But the guardians didn't bleed. And they didn't tire.

"We're not gonna win this," she hissed, breath fogging.

Not like this.

But then.
A flare of energy surged through her, not from rage, or fear, but from the Fold itself. The veil between worlds *stirred* in her chest, something inside her responding to the presence of the guardians.

They froze mid-step.

All five.

Their molten eyes flicked to Isla, and then, as one, they knelt.

The mists grew thicker, swirling, until a voice not born of flesh rumbled from the stones themselves:

"Touched by the Veil… bearer of paths unseen. You walk between the laws of the old and new."

Isla's breath caught.

"I don't understand."

"You are known," said the voice, now emanating from the guardian directly before her. "The Fold remembers. Few bear its mark and survive. Fewer still are not devoured."

Ronan, halfway between wolf and man, stared. "What mark?"

Isla raised her palm. There, faint, glowing now with soft, silvery light, was the outline of the rune from the tunnels. The same sigil that had whispered to her in her dreams since that dreaded night at seabright. The same one Elias couldn't trace in any book.

She looked back at the guardians. "We don't seek the Crown to rule," she said, voice steady. "We need it to stop something worse. A vampire named Katerina is turning humans, breaking the old laws, risking exposure of the entire supernatural world. She wants power, not peace. And the things she's stirring... they go beyond this realm."

The guardians didn't move.

"I give you my word," Isla pressed on, louder now, voice like steel. "We will return the Crown to the Fold when it's no longer needed. I will bear it, and no one else. Let it bind to me, until this is done."

Silence.

Then, slowly, the guardians rose. One stepped forward, towering, and held out a massive, stone hand.

"Then the pact is made."

The air shimmered as the cloth unravelled from the dais, the Crown of Ash rising into the air on its own. It hovered before Isla, forged of dark iron and bone, etched with glyphs that shifted like smoke, pulsing with restrained power.

She reached out, hand steady, and touched it. It seared her palm. Pain flared like fire through her body, but she didn't let go.

She gritted her teeth, eyes blazing gold, and pressed forward.

The Crown sank against her chest, not onto her head, but into her, bonding with her blood, her bones. The symbols glowed across her skin before fading, like tattoos burnt into memory.

Then the mist lifted. The guardians faded. The Fold exhaled.

And Isla stood. Trembling and steady all at once.

Ronan approached, his shift complete, eyes wide. "You alright?"

"Not even close," she muttered. "But I have it."

They turned together, and as they stepped beyond the stones of Dunn's Fold, the wind carried a whisper behind them:

"Only the worthy may rise. But all who rise must one day fall."

Chapter 25: Marked by Ash

The safehouse was quiet, thick with the kind of silence that comes after something irreversible.

Isla stood in the middle of the room, her shirt torn down the centre, the skin beneath still faintly smoking. Black, branch-like veins curled outward from a jagged sigil branded directly over her sternum, the Crown of Ash, not worn, but *embedded*. Not carved. Not burned.

Claimed.

No one spoke at first. Not even Ronan.

Camilla was the first to move, stepping forward slowly with a horrified look on her face. "Okay," she said cautiously, gesturing to Isla's chest. "So… that's normal now?"

Isla exhaled shakily. The pain had dulled to a distant throb, but she still felt it, a heavy presence beneath her skin, like something ancient curled up inside her ribcage, *waiting*.

"No," she said. "It's not."

Elias was pacing near the bookshelves, flipping through one of his older tomes with fingers that twitched like they couldn't move fast enough. "It's not supposed to do that," he muttered, more to himself than to the room. "The crown was symbolic, a vessel of power, yes, but... it was always passed, held. *Separate*. This, this is something else."

"It knew her," Ronan said quietly. "The guardians didn't hesitate. They recognized her."

"Because she's got history with creepy supernatural symbols lighting her up like a damn rave?" Camilla asked. "Or because this was always going to happen?"

Isla didn't answer. She didn't have to.

Elias stopped pacing. "The veil," he said. "It's the only thing that makes sense. She crossed it once before, Seabright. That place left a mark on her. I didn't realize how deep it ran."

"That was years ago," Isla said, voice low. "I survived it. Barely. I didn't bring anything back."

"Didn't you?" Elias asked, his tone gentler now. "You returned... different. No one walks through the veil and comes back untouched. You didn't just survive the Hollow One, Isla. You crossed into its domain and lived. And now... the crown knows you."

Ronan stepped closer to Isla, his eyes drawn to the dark mark etched across her chest. "This isn't just power. It's a tether to the other side."

Isla looked down at the symbol, the way the edges glowed faintly with embers that never fully dimmed. "It didn't give me a choice."

"It never does," Elias said grimly. "This isn't a weapon. It's a *pact*. It's the weight of balance. You're not just a bearer now, Isla, you are the covenant."

Camilla blinked. "Okay, hold up. So she's like the magical fail-safe guardian of reality or something?"

"Not exactly," Elias replied. "But if she misuses the power, if the balance tips too far in one direction, who knows what it could bring back to fight."

"Again," Camilla muttered. "Why do we keep giving the fate of the world to the emotionally compromised werewolf with rage issues?"

Ronan almost smiled. "Because she's the only one strong enough to carry it."

Isla met his gaze, something unreadable flickering in her expression. "I didn't ask for this."

"No one ever does," Elias said. "But that doesn't change what it means."

"What *does* it mean?" Camilla asked, looking between them. "What happens now?"

Isla pulled her shirt closed, wincing as the fabric brushed over the still-hot mark. Her voice, when she spoke, was quiet, but certain.

"It means we don't have time to fail."

Elias nodded slowly, eyes narrowing with thought. "Then we find the rest of Katerina's plans. Whatever she's trying to unearth, whatever power she's chasing, we stop it before it wakes something that *can't* be put back."

"And if it's already awake?" Ronan asked.

Isla looked out the cracked window, where dusk had begun bleeding across the sky like spilled ink.

"Then we make sure it remembers why it should be afraid of us."

Camilla gave Isla a lingering look, eyes flicking down to the still-faintly-glowing mark, then over to Elias with a sigh. "Well, while our girl was out here branding herself with ancient vampire artifacts, Elias and I were doing something radical, like research."

Elias rolled his eyes. "She means she complained for two hours while I did the research."

Camilla grinned. "Semantics."

Isla chuckled under her breath. The warmth of the moment, however brief, cut through the heavy sense of dread that still clung to her.

Camilla reached into her satchel and pulled out a thick folder, dropping it onto the table with a dramatic thump. "So. We traced the symbols found near the feral nest and cross-referenced them with some of the etchings Elias and I found in a creepy tunnel"

"Codex," Elias corrected.

"Tomb," she insisted, ignoring him. "Turns out, they're not just decoration. They're territorial glyphs. Markers. The kind vampires used during the last Great War to lay claim to underground sanctuaries and strongholds."

Elias picked up where she left off. "And the ones we found in the Peak District, the tunnels... they weren't just remnants. They were recently redrawn. Someone's reclaiming those old spaces. Katerina is trying to restore, or mimic, the structure of the old vampire courts."

"She's building something," Isla murmured. "A kingdom."

"Or an army," Camilla said. "Complete with power bases and escape routes. If we're right, then the tunnels we explored are just the tip of it. She's mapping out territory across the city."

"Like she's preparing for a siege," Elias added. "Not just to seize power but to hold it."

Isla nodded slowly. "Which means she's not planning on running. She's planning on ruling."

Camilla shot her a sly grin. "So, let me get this straight. You got half-singed by a mystical relic and now you're carrying it inside you like some walking apocalypse egg. Should I be worried you're going to sprout shadow wings again? Or maybe breathe fire this time?"

Isla smirked. "I make no promises."

Elias chuckled, though his gaze was thoughtful. "Joking aside, Camilla might be onto something. The crown wasn't just symbolic power, it was protective. It could influence the flow of magic, create barriers, manipulate energies tied to the veil. You might find yourself… altered."

"Great," Isla muttered. "Because being a werewolf wasn't enough."

Ronan leaned against the doorway, arms crossed, watching her with a quiet intensity. "Whatever you are now, you're still you."

"Yeah," Camilla added, nudging her shoulder. "Just… slightly more terrifying and glowy."

Elias spread the ancient map he'd recovered across the table. "We found one more thing. There's mention of a convergence point, beneath the old Roman foundations. Near Castlefield. The glyphs all seem to direct toward it."

"It might be her seat of power," he continued. "Or where she intends to complete whatever ritual she's working toward. If we get there first, we might stand a chance at understanding the full scale of her plan."

Isla looked around the room at her team, her pack, in every way that mattered. She touched the mark on her chest, feeling the slow, steady pulse beneath her skin. Power. Responsibility. A war that hadn't yet been declared but was already being fought in blood and shadow.

"Then let's finish this," she said. "Before she builds something that can't be torn down."

And somewhere, far beneath the streets of Manchester, Katerina opened her eyes, and smiled.

Chapter 26: Queen of Ash and Blood

Katerina stood at the edge of the underground crypt, bathed in the cold amber glow of firelight reflecting off damp stone. The cavernous chamber beneath Castlefield, long lost to the city above, pulsed with residual energy, old power, ancient bloodlines, and something older still, whispering from the cracks in the stone. The convergence point.

Around her, her new brood waited, ferals and faithful alike. Some crouched, twitching in the shadows, their minds half-broken from the turning. Others stood upright, eyes gleaming with unnatural focus. They were her experiments. Her army. And though not all had survived the turning, those who did were stronger, faster... crueller.

Not perfect, no, but useful.

Katerina's hand brushed the obsidian table that had once served as a war council's seat during the vampire uprising centuries ago. Time had buried it, dust and decay trying to erase the memory of what they once were. But she was done hiding in the shadows, done bowing to Elders who feared the humans more than they feared the hunger in their own veins.

"Soon," she whispered, fingers trailing across a carved symbol, older than vampire, older than anything that should exist in this realm. "The city will remember what it is to fear the dark."

A flicker of movement caught her attention. One of her lieutenants, a vampire named Alric, stepped from the shadows and bowed his head. His eyes glinted with reverence... and just the right amount of fear.

"My lady. Three more turned in Ancoats. Two survived. The third... burned from the inside out."

Katerina frowned. "The blood was wrong?"

"No. He resisted. Fought too hard."

She exhaled sharply. "Then he was weak. Leave the body as a warning."

Alric nodded. "And the ones near Deansgate?"

"Unleash them," she said, her voice cold and sharp. "Let the humans panic. Let the wolves and witches chase shadows while we carve our path beneath their feet."

Alric hesitated, then added, "The Alpha and the detective... they survived the assault at the estate."

Katerina's jaw tensed. "Of course they did." She turned slowly, the firelight dancing across her porcelain features, eyes glowing faintly with the telltale shine of hunger. "Crowley is becoming a thorn."

Alric's voice lowered. "She bears something new. There's talk… whispers among the ferals that she carries the mark of the crown."

Katerina stilled.

So, the crown had accepted her?

Interesting.

Infuriating.

"Then she's more dangerous than I thought." Her smile turned feral. "Good. Let her come for me. Let them all come. The crown was forged in ash and blood, it can just as easily be broken in it."

She moved through the chamber, past twisted murals of forgotten vampire lineages and toward the tunnel that led even deeper, where the air grew heavier, and the veil between realms thinned. Behind her, her ferals shifted and hissed, sensing her intent. The glyphs pulsed faintly on the stone.

The ritual she'd begun weeks ago was nearly complete. Her claim would not just be over Manchester. It would stretch through every bloodline that had dared to forget her name.

Let the Elders sit on their crumbling thrones.

Let the wolves clutch their fading power.

Let the girl with the crown burn herself trying to stop her.

Katerina stepped into the heart of the chamber where the final symbol waited to be awakened, her voice low and full of venom.

"The age of secrecy is ending. It's time for the world to remember why it feared the dark."

And above her, in the city of glass and brick, the shadows stirred.

Chapter 27: Blood in the Streets

The night air was thick with tension. Sirens wailed in the distance, their shrill cry echoing off the glass and steel of Manchester's skyline as Isla crouched beside the mutilated body dumped in the alley off Ancoats.

It was meant to be a message. Not just a kill, an exhibition.

The victim's body had been splayed open, ribs cracked wide as if torn from the inside. The chest cavity was hollow. Drained. Not just of blood, but of everything human. Someone had burned a symbol into the concrete beside the body, a jagged spiral with a crown-like slash at the centre. It pulsed with residual energy, the mark of something ancient and angry.

Isla stared at it, her breath coming slow and controlled. She could feel it in her bones, this wasn't just murder. It was a declaration.

Behind her, Camilla swore under her breath. "Jesus, they left him like an offering."

"Or a warning," Elias muttered, running a gloved hand along the symbol. "This isn't just vampire bravado. This is ritualistic."

"Which means she's accelerating," Isla said, standing. Her voice was low, steady, but the growl beneath her words betrayed the tension threading through her chest. "She's not hiding anymore. She wants to shake the city."

"And she's doing it." Camilla pointed down the alley to the chaos spilling onto the street beyond, screams, crashing glass, the thud of something large and fast hitting a car roof.

The ferals had arrived.

One tore through the crowd on all fours, a blur of pale limbs and blood-streaked teeth. People ran in every direction, a few falling before they could scream. The feral launched itself at a fleeing woman, but Isla moved first.

With a snap of motion, she shifted, eyes glowing amber, claws extending just enough, and intercepted the vampire mid-air, slamming it into the pavement with a crack. Her strength surged unnaturally, pulsing from the brand burned into her chest.

The feral hissed, mouth stretching wider than any human jaw could, until Elias stepped in and drove a silver dagger through its throat. The creature shrieked, convulsed, and then stilled, smoke curling from the wound.

Ronan joined from the flank, his clothes already bloodied. "There's more coming in from the side streets. We have to contain them or they'll tear the city apart."

Camilla lifted her pistol, loaded with UV rounds Elias had made for her. "Then let's do what we do best."

They moved fast, Isla leading with preternatural grace, Ronan flanking like a war-born shadow, Elias casting sigils mid-stride, and Camilla holding the line with precision and grit. The fight stretched across the alleyways and walkways, a coordinated chaos of strikes, bites, bullets, and spellfire.

One feral tried to drag a bleeding man into a stairwell but Isla lunged, catching it by the throat and slamming it back with enough force to shatter concrete. Another clawed at Elias, only to be blown back by a burst of kinetic energy from a runestone he hadn't used in years.

Still, they kept coming.

"They're not even turning to flee," Ronan growled, slashing through one. "She's driving them like weapons. They don't care if they survive."

"They're not meant to survive," Isla said. "They're distractions."

Just then, her comm crackled.

"Unit Six, report. We've got fires breaking out along the tram line. Confirmed injuries at two more scenes."

Camilla answered, trying to sound as detached and professional as always. "We're on scene. Multiple perpetrators. Possible drug-induced frenzy."

It was the official story they'd seeded, feral vampires masquerading as rage-fuelled addicts, a growing "underground cult" that had begun to break through to the surface.

Isla clenched her jaw. "This is the beginning. She's softening us up."

Ronan's expression was grim. "We need to strike back. Now."

Elias straightened, his voice urgent. "No. We need to understand what she's doing with that symbol. The ritual, the blood. She's not just trying to rule, she's trying to tear down the rules."

Isla turned back to the branded spiral in the concrete, still faintly glowing.

Katerina wasn't just making war.

She was rewriting the law of the supernatural.

If they didn't stop her soon, there wouldn't be a city left to save, only ash, blood, and a crown worn by a mad queen.

Chapter 28: Ash and Fire

The city was unravelling.

The sharp scent of blood and smoke hung thick in the night air as Isla leapt over a burning barricade, boots crunching on broken glass and scorched tarmac. Her lungs burned, not just from the heat, but from the weight of it all, the screams echoing through the narrow backstreets, the hollowed-out silence that followed each one.

Behind her, Camilla barked into a police radio, still doing what she could to maintain their cover. "Unit Nine, do not engage. I repeat, do not engage. Wait for tactical backup. Suspects are considered unstable and highly violent."

The code was wearing thin. Too many unexplained deaths. Too many witnesses whispering about glowing eyes and creatures moving faster than the eye could track. It wouldn't hold forever.

From the shadows, another feral lunged.

This one was faster. Smarter.

Isla barely caught its scent before it struck, claws raking through the air as she twisted sideways and rammed a silver knife beneath its chin. It howled, the sound almost human. Almost.

Elias flanked her, his coat flaring as he hurled a protective ward just in time to block a second feral rushing from the side. It struck the barrier and burst into flames, his modified sigils were getting more aggressive, more precise.

"I counted five more," he said breathlessly, voice tight. "She's not just releasing them. She's *placing* them."

"What do you mean?" Ronan called over his shoulder as he drove a dagger through a creature's chest and spun to face another.

"They're too spaced out, too strategic. It's not random. They're herded into zones. Like she's carving paths through the city." Elias crouched to sketch something into the grime with a chalked fingertip. "There's a pattern. It's not just chaos, it's a *map*."

Isla's stomach turned. "To what?"

Elias met her gaze, eyes dark with dread. "To something buried. Or something locked away."

They didn't speak the next thought aloud.

Something Katerina was trying to bring back.

Something old.

Something powerful.

Something *forbidden*.

Camilla swore softly, sliding beside Isla with her sidearm drawn. "Okay, can we stop resurrecting ancient horrors for, like, five minutes?"

A low growl rumbled in Isla's chest, not from humour. "It's not just resurrection. It's power consolidation. She's feeding the city to something. Feeding it to wake something up."

Ronan sheathed his bloodied blade, his breathing heavy but steady. "If she's using blood rituals to tear open the old pathways."

"She's trying to reforge a connection to the *first court*," Elias finished grimly. "The bloodline before modern vampire law. The ones erased from history after the old wars."

Isla turned slowly. "The ones exiled beyond the Veil."

Camilla's brows furrowed. "You mean, like, *the* ancient vampires? Boogeyman-level bad?"

"Worse," Elias muttered. "They weren't just exiled. They were *sealed*. If she's trying to bring them back…"

"She's risking annihilation for the sake of a throne," Ronan growled.

"No," Isla said quietly. "She's planning to share her crown."

The silence fell like a guillotine.

They stood there, panting amid the ruin, with the city bleeding behind them and the sky overhead beginning to cloud with a storm that wasn't made of weather. Somewhere deep beneath Manchester's foundations, power was shifting. Old power. Hungry power.

Isla's hand drifted to her chest, where the Crown of Ash pulsed faintly under her skin like a second heartbeat. She could feel it reacting to the surge, the imbalance. The call of something ancient scratching at the seams of reality.

"She's further along than we thought," Elias said. "If she breaks that seal, if she brings one of them back."

"She won't," Isla said. Her voice was low, rough with certainty. "We stop her before that happens."

Camilla blew out a breath. "Great. No pressure."

Isla looked at each of them, Ronan with blood crusted along his cheekbone, Elias' chalk-stained hands trembling from spell work, and Camilla, still somehow holding the line between the supernatural and the world she was born in.

"We don't stop this, the war the world forgot comes back. The Veil falls. And Manchester becomes ground zero."

Ronan stepped forward, gripping her shoulder. "Then we hit her now. No more hunting shadows. We bring the fight to her."

Isla nodded. "Agreed. But we do it smart."

"We'll need allies," Elias said. "Old ones."

Isla nodded again. "Then let's go remind the old blood that if they want their secrets kept and their world protected, they'd better stand with us. Or burn with her."

Chapter 29: The Gathering Storm

The council chamber of the vampire elders was colder than it had any right to be, considering the blood that had been spilled to build it.

Tucked beneath the foundations of the old John Rylands Library, the ancient hall still reeked faintly of parchment, wax, and arrogance. Stone pillars rose like petrified limbs in a silent forest, casting long shadows that stretched over Isla's boots as she stepped forward, chin high despite the weight in her chest.

They had come back. Not by choice, by necessity.

Three elders stood before them, unmoved and unimpressed: Lady Halvara, her skin like glass over bone; Chancellor Morrick, all measured cruelty behind his smile; and the silent one, simply called Sable, who never spoke, only watched with the eerie stillness of a predator who had no need for words.

Ronan flanked Isla, arms crossed, tension in every line of his broad frame. Elias stood slightly behind; fingers laced before him like a scholar presenting a thesis rather than a war warning. Camilla kept to Isla's left, hands shoved in her coat, eyes scanning the chamber with thinly veiled distrust.

"You were warned," Morrick said smoothly. "We told you that if you engaged Katerina outside of sanctioned trial, the court would not intervene."

"We're not asking you to fight our battle," Isla said evenly. "We're showing you the battlefield you're choosing to ignore."

Elias stepped forward and unfurled a series of maps, placing them on the marble table between them. "These are the confirmed attack zones. Bodies found drained, ferals spotted. Symbols carved into stone and skin, older than the court, predating the exile."

He tapped a sigil etched in blood. "This appeared at three sites. It's the mark of the Ash Crown, the crest of the lost court. The ones you buried."

Lady Halvara's gaze flickered to the mark and held there just a second too long.

"You know what she's trying to do," Isla said. "You feel the imbalance already. The wards on your own tombs are weakening."

Still, the elders remained silent.

Ronan growled low. "Are you going to stand there and do nothing while she tears your world apart? She's not just turning humans anymore. She's trying to *wake* something."

Sable tilted their head. Finally, a voice broke the silence. It was Lady Halvara's, crisp and dispassionate.

"You seek to provoke the old blood. The sealed lords were banished for a reason. Their resurrection would mean the end of this fragile peace, and your kind, wolf, would burn first."

"And *your kind* would follow," Elias said flatly. "You think you'll survive an ancient power reclaiming its throne? Katerina doesn't want balance. She wants dominion. And she doesn't care how many of you she slaughters to get it."

Camilla stepped forward, surprising them all. "You think hiding behind tradition is noble? It's cowardice. If you won't stop her, then get out of our way."

Lady Halvara's eyes gleamed, amused. "You have spirit, little human."

"She has more courage than most who call this place home," Isla snapped. "You say the law protects you. The law was built to protect the world from you. You want to remain hidden? Then do something. Or when the ash falls, it'll fall on your graves too."

A long silence stretched between them. Then Morrick stepped forward.

"You will have no army from us. No public declaration. But…"

A sliver of parchment was pushed across the table.

"A name. An exile. One of the old ones who refused to take a side during the last war. He lives on the edge of the Veil, forgotten by most. If anyone remembers the rites Katerina is trying to complete, it would be him."

"What's the catch?" Elias asked warily.

Morrick smiled. "He's not loyal to *any* court. And he hates wolves."

Camilla smirked. "Great. So basically Tuesday."

Ronan grunted. "Give us the name."

They left the chamber with more tension than answers, but a path, nonetheless.

Back at the safehouse, they laid everything out. Maps. Timelines. Blood patterns. Symbol placement. From a distance, the web of Katerina's chaos began to resemble something more coherent.

"She's triangulating something," Elias murmured. "This is ritual construction. Massive scale. She's building a gateway. But not just one to pull something through, it's a *throne*. She's summoning a lord to sit in it."

"And she's going to let the city burn to light the way," Isla said grimly.

The location was clear now. The final point of power sat beneath Manchester Cathedral, where ley lines converged, and a forgotten crypt remained sealed since the time of the Black Death.

Isla traced her finger across the map. "That's where it ends."

Camilla looked up. "Or where we end it."

Elias nodded slowly. "Then we need allies. We need weapons. We need that exile."

Ronan glanced at Isla. "We'll find him. And if he refuses?"

Isla's eyes darkened, the mark of the Ash Crown glowing faintly beneath her collarbone. "Then he'll learn what it means to face someone who walked the Veil and survived."

Outside, the wind picked up. In the distance, thunder rolled across the moors like war drums. The final battle was coming. And this time, they wouldn't be hunting shadows.

Chapter 30: The One Who Remained

They found the exile far from the city, beyond the reach of ley lines, buried in the fractured cliffs of Alderley Edge, where the rocks themselves whispered old truths. It was a place steeped in folklore, known to humans as a landscape of legends. But those who walked the Veil knew better. It was a boundary, scarred by forgotten battles and sealed betrayals.

Elias had followed the threads of rumour and records, tracing spells encoded in long-dead dialects to a single name: Vaelric.

A fae once bound to the highest court, now cast out for refusing to kneel to war.

"I don't like this," Camilla muttered as they hiked the narrow trail between slabs of stone that jutted from the earth like broken teeth. "Feels like walking into a trap wrapped in a fairy tale."

"Welcome to the fae," Elias said grimly. "Everything's a test. Every word's a contract. And nothing is ever what it seems."

Ronan walked ahead, eyes sharp, muscles tense beneath his shirt. "I can smell him. He's old. Strong."

Isla could feel it too, magic that thrummed beneath her skin like a distant drum. Her mark, the Crown now part of her, pulsed faintly in time with the beat. It was as if the land itself recognized it... or feared it.

They reached the stone archway nestled between the rocks, carved with sigils that bled silver under the light. The wind stilled. Time bent.

And then he appeared.

Vaelric.

He stepped through the shimmer of air without sound, tall and draped in robes made from starlight and shadow. His eyes, burning gold, passed over each of them with detached indifference... until they landed on Isla.

"A wolf," he said coldly, his voice ancient and ageless. "You dare bring a beast to my domain."

Ronan bristled, fangs flashing. "Say that again."

Isla raised a hand, stopping him. "I'm not here as part of the Pack," she said. "I'm not here as a hunter. I came because something is rising, and it threatens all of us."

Vaelric's gaze narrowed. "And why should that concern me? I made no vows to the vampires or your kind."

Elias stepped forward, tone respectful but firm. "Because Katerina is awakening a throne long buried, one sealed by your own ancestors. She's trying to undo what you once refused to join."

Vaelric gave no reaction, but Isla felt the shift in the air.

Still, it wasn't enough.

"You seek to manipulate me," he said. "You come here with no offering, no rite, no respect for the law of the old blood. Why should I not strike you down where you stand?"

Isla stepped forward slowly.

And unfastened the collar of her shirt just enough to reveal the mark, burned into her skin, etched in power older than kingdoms.

The Crown of Ash.

Vaelric froze.

Silence stretched thick and heavy as the wind returned, whispering through the rocks like voices of the dead.

"You wear the mark," he said finally, voice low and reverent. "But you are not kin to those who forged it. You are wolf-blooded. Mortal-born."

"I crossed the Veil," Isla said. "I faced what lies beyond. And it chose not to devour me."

"She's been marked to protect," Elias added. "She doesn't serve one side of the war. She's trying to stop a new one before it begins."

Vaelric studied her, long and hard. His lip curled faintly, but it was no longer contempt.

"Perhaps… you are not as unworthy as you seem."

He turned, robes swirling, and beckoned them into his sanctum, a hidden space beneath the stones, where ancient glyphs glowed and tomes levitated midair.

"You came for knowledge," Vaelric said. "I will give you what I know. But understand this, Isla Crowley. The Crown has chosen you… but it will consume you if you do not wield it carefully. Its power was never meant to serve the balance. Only to restore dominance when all else fails."

"What happens if I use it to kill her?" Isla asked.

He looked at her then, truly looked. And in his ancient eyes, she saw what it meant to carry fire in your veins.

"Then you must become more than wolf. More than woman. You must become the force that brings peace… or war."

A cold tremor ran down her spine.

And somewhere beyond the cliffs, far in the city's heart, the sky split with a crack of thunder.

Katerina had made her next move.

They were running out of time.

They sat in silence beneath the stone canopy of Vaelric's sanctum.

Flickering glyphs floated like drifting constellations in the air, each a memory, a spell, a buried truth. Ancient books were stacked with reverence, their covers stitched from hide that had never belonged to any beast in this world.

Vaelric poured a dark, thick liquid into carved cups, his version of hospitality, bitter and spiced with something that made Camilla immediately gag and whisper to Elias, "Why is everything in this world either glowing, cursed, or tastes like actual hell?"

The fae ignored her.

Instead, he lowered himself into a seat carved into the roots of a petrified tree that had long since turned to obsidian, eyes steady on Isla.

"You want to know why I didn't fight in the last war," he said, as if the question had hung between them all along. "Why I let the world burn and bled for no kingdom."

Isla met his gaze. "If you knew what was coming, why didn't you try to stop it?"

Vaelric's smile was faint. Sad. "Because the last war was never meant to be won. Not truly. It was a cleansing, not a conquest. A reckoning brought upon our kind by our own hubris."

He flicked a finger, and images formed in the air, shadows of a history long buried.

Flashes of bloodied skies.

Mountains weeping fire.

Rows upon rows of vampires, feral and maddened, clashing against beasts twisted by ancient magic. Fae armies wrapped in armour of living moonlight. Shattered human cities that never made the history books.

"The vampires were fractured," he continued. "As they always are. Too many covens. Too many kings. One sought to unify them. To wear the crown forged from ash and bone. But it was never meant to rule... only to burn. The fae tried to destroy it. But someone, *something*, protected it."

"Something from the other side," Elias murmured.

Vaelric nodded. "The Veil is not a wall. It is a scar. And something lives in the wound."

A long silence followed.

Camilla stared into her untouched cup. "Okay, that's comforting."

"I stayed out of the war because I saw the truth," Vaelric said. "No one side was just. Not the vampires. Not the fae. Not the wolves, who tried to fight for peace but were torn apart by their own instincts. I watched kingdoms rise and fall for nothing but ego and blood. I stayed alive, so someone would remember."

Isla felt the Crown's mark burn gently against her chest, like it was listening. Ronan shifted beside her. "But if Katerina is trying to bring that war back…"

"Then she is either a fool," Vaelric said, "or she serves something far more dangerous."

He stood and moved toward a shelf lined with shards of crystal and bone.

"You want to stop her? Then you cannot fight her with your Pack. Or the court. They have forgotten what's at stake. You must gather those who still remember." He pulled a single scroll free, wrapped in a silken cloth that shimmered like mist.

"And you must not lose control of the Crown."

"What happens if I do?" Isla asked, voice steady.

Vaelric turned, and in the glow of the sanctum's light, the truth hung between them like a blade.

"Then you will become her."

The air thickened with the weight of it. Not threat. Not prophecy. Possibility.

They left the sanctum with more than they'd come for, knowledge, warnings, and an uneasy ally who had seen too many wars to believe blindly in heroes.

But something in the way Vaelric watched Isla as she walked away told her that *maybe*, just maybe, he believed in her.

Even if he'd never say it out loud.

Chapter 31: Queen of the Fallen

The chamber beneath the cathedral was cloaked in silence. A cold, undisturbed kind that made the air feel like it hadn't been breathed in centuries. It was here that Katerina stood, alone, surrounded by relics stolen from the long-dead leaders of the Old War, symbols of blood, betrayal, and sacrifice.

Candles flickered in perfect formation, arranged to mirror a sigil carved into the black stone floor. Ancient. Forbidden. Older than even the Veil itself.

The blood of her latest offering sizzled as it met the carving's deepest grooves.

The ritual was nearly complete.

Katerina tilted her head back, crimson eyes glinting with a wild, simmering pride. "You called us monsters," she whispered into the shadows. "But we were always the apex. The gods beneath the flesh. And now, they will remember."

Behind her, footsteps echoed.

The vampire known only as Alric stepped into view, her most loyal creation. The first to survive her turning without unravelling into madness.

He knelt. "The ferals have sown chaos through the city. The humans are beginning to believe the rage drug is a bio-terror attack. Their news channels are erupting. Panic is growing."

Katerina smiled.

"Good," she said. "Panic turns law to ash. Once fear takes root, they'll welcome any order that promises peace."

"And the wolves?"

"They'll cling to balance until the city is rubble," she said coldly. "Even Isla Crowley. Especially her."

Her lip curled slightly as she moved to the pedestal where a scroll, bound in chains of silver and bone, sat untouched for centuries. Her hand hovered above it, fingertips trembling.

"They locked this away after the Old War. A weapon forged from the blood of their own gods, cursed by the Fae, hidden by their Elders. But they forgot one thing." She turned to Alric, eyes blazing. "The dead do not stay buried when someone remembers their name."

Alric didn't respond. He knew better.

"What of the Crown?" he asked instead. "The wolves have it."

"No," she said sharply. "*She* has it."

Katerina's tone was low, dangerous. "Isla. The one touched by the Veil."

She moved slowly to a mirror, its surface rippling with shadows, not reflection. There, in a brief glimmer of light, Isla's face flickered like a ghost.

"She's powerful. Too powerful. But she doesn't know how to wield what she's been given." Her fingers clenched at her sides. "The Crown chose her because of her bloodline... but the Veil marks more than just strength. It marks those willing to sacrifice everything."

Katerina turned back to the circle. "So we make her sacrifice everything. Her friends. Her Pack. Her city. And when she's broken... the true heir will rise."

She stepped into the centre of the circle. The chains broke with a whisper of wind, and the scroll lifted from its resting place.

"Tonight," she said, voice rising, "we awaken the gate beneath the city. And when it opens... the bloodbound covenant will shatter."

Alric stepped back as the shadows around the chamber began to pulse with movement, figures forming in the gloom, not fully human, not fully anything.

"You will not rule," one of them rasped.

"I don't want to rule," Katerina replied. "I want to erase the world that cast us out."

The sigil flared to life beneath Katerina's feet, casting an unnatural crimson glow that pulsed in time with her heartbeat.

Then came the whispers.

Not voices, not truly. They hissed around the room like wind through a crypt, brushing her skin and stealing the warmth from the air.

Figures stepped out of the shadows.

There were six in total, each cloaked in veils of darkness so complete it seemed the light bent around them. Not illusions. Not ghosts. But remnants, echoes bound to blood and memory. Sentinels tied to the Old War.

Guardians of the Lineage.

They had once been vampires, long before the Laws, before civility, before the world had names for things that walked by moonlight and killed without remorse. Now they were something less... and more. A council that existed in memory only, stirred by the activation of a sigil that hadn't been touched in nearly a thousand years.

"You awaken what should remain buried," one rasped, its voice a hollow hum in the marrow of her bones.

"I awaken our birthright," Katerina spat, defiant.

"You do not understand what you call," another said, stepping forward. His face was a hollowed-out echo, blurred and burned by time. "The Blood Throne was not left vacant by mistake. He was entombed, Katerina."

Katerina's eyes narrowed. "Vaelric sealed him away. Out of fear."

"No. Out of mercy," the hollow figure replied. "The one you seek to raise was not a ruler. He was a *weapon*. A curse in flesh. The Crown of Ash burned through armies not to protect, but to consume."

Katerina's lips curled into a smirk. "And I will use that curse to reshape this broken world."

Another stepped forward, this one female, her voice soft but no less chilling. "You think to control him? Bend him to your will?"

Katerina didn't answer.

"You would be ash before you spoke his name aloud."

"I've already spoken it," she said. "I've carved it into the city's foundations. I've turned its people into my army. I've shed the blood of Elder and newborn alike in his name."

The temperature dropped. Alric shifted uneasily behind her.

"You cannot rule what was forged in the First Turning," the woman said. "He is no longer a vampire. He is hunger. Rage. Vengeance bound in immortal flesh."

"I am not afraid of what he is," Katerina snapped. "Because I *am* what he is. You locked away the apex of our kind because you grew weak. Because you wanted peace. But peace is a lie told by those afraid of power."

A long silence followed.

Then the first figure stepped forward once more, cloaked in deepest black, its voice now quiet with something colder than anger, sorrow.

"You are not his queen," it said.

Katerina raised her chin.

"No," she whispered, eyes glowing like twin embers. "I will be his *heir*."

The circle blazed hotter. The figures began to fade, dissolving into shadow, leaving one final warning etched into the air between them.

"What is buried remembers. And what remembers… hungers."

When the light faded, the chamber was still.

Alric approached slowly, careful not to touch the now-seared floor. "What happens now?" he asked.

Katerina turned toward the mirror again, and this time, it did not show Isla.

It showed a stone gate, half buried beneath centuries of ruin, marked with the sigil of the Blood Throne. A gate beneath the city. Beneath Manchester. A place long forgotten.

"We find the tomb," Katerina said. "We raise the First."

Chapter 32: Smoke and Mirrors

Manchester's skyline was dull against the early morning haze, a grey wash of buildings, light drizzle, and blurred sirens in the distance. It could've been any ordinary day. But Isla knew better.

She and Camilla stood outside the precinct, coffee in hand, both watching the swarm of officers move in and out of the double glass doors. Inside, the world spun on, oblivious to the war festering beneath their feet.

"Still want to be a detective, Mills?" Isla asked, sipping her coffee without looking at her partner.

Camilla huffed a breath, tugging her coat tighter around her shoulders. "I wanted weird. I just didn't think weird would mean bloodthirsty vampires, a magic crown welded to your chest, and death cults under Deansgate."

"Careful," Isla smirked, "you're starting to sound like Elias."

"Ugh. Shoot me now."

They stepped inside, weaving through the main corridor, nodding at familiar faces. They needed to keep up appearances. Needed to stay ahead of the narrative. The media was still spinning the "designer drug" line, and they had to make sure that stuck long enough to move on Katerina without the whole city panicking.

In the incident room, Isla dropped a folder onto the whiteboard table while Camilla powered up the touchscreen map on the wall. Red pins marked every murder and attack site in the last two weeks. The board looked like a battlefield.

And in a way, it was.

"Alright," Isla said, voice low as she flicked through reports. "Let's look at it from both angles. Human and supernatural."

Camilla nodded, pulling out the murder files. "All the bodies we've recovered from the last three nights, same trauma. Torn throats, drained blood, but some variation in methods. That's what's weird."

"Turned vamps," Isla murmured. "Some fresh. Some unstable. Katerina's not being careful anymore, she's turning people faster, trying to build an army."

"She's losing control of them."

"Or she doesn't care if she does."

Camilla clicked a few settings and pulled up surveillance footage from outside one of the scenes.

"We might have something here. CCTV caught someone watching the alley two nights ago. Pale. Hooded. Didn't move even when the sirens rolled in."

Isla leaned in. "Damn. Freeze that. Enhance if you can."

The grainy image sharpened just enough to reveal a shadowed face. Too far to ID, but Isla's wolf instincts prickled.

"That's one of hers," she whispered.

"Think she's scouting?"

"No," Isla replied. "I think they're marking places. Preparing them. Every attack has been in places tied to the city's old ley lines. Katerina's not just turning people, she's circling something."

Camilla's lips tightened. "You mean the crypt? That gate?"

Isla nodded. "Whatever she's trying to raise… she's building toward it. These murders feel like she's building a boundary."

"Then where does it point to?"

Isla pulled out an old map Elias had marked weeks ago, overlaying the ley lines and attack sites. As the pieces aligned, the pattern became unmistakable.

"They're converging beneath the old cathedral ruins," Isla said slowly. "There's a sublevel, half-collapsed during the bombings. Elias mentioned it once, part of the underground crypt system older than the city itself."

Camilla stared at the board. "So that's where we strike?"

Isla's jaw clenched. "It's where we *try*. But we need Ronan and Elias. We hit that place, we're walking into her den."

As if summoned, Isla's phone buzzed.

A message from Elias: "Vaelric's tale has more teeth than we thought. We're heading back now. Meet at the safehouse."

"Looks like the boys found something too," Isla muttered. "Let's wrap up here. We'll plant some new leads for the department, keep them focused on the drug ring, suggest a rival gang escalation. Make it messy. Confusing. Just enough to cover the truth."

Camilla smirked. "Smoke and mirrors. I'm getting good at this supernatural spy game."

Isla grabbed the files. "Let's just hope we're still breathing when it's over."

They left the precinct as the city swirled behind them, unaware that war loomed beneath their feet.

Chapter 33: Threads Pulled Tight

The scent of antiseptic clung to Isla's coat, her senses sharper than ever since the Crown had marked her. It pulsed beneath her skin like a second heartbeat, a whisper of ancient power curled in the hollow of her collarbone. She kept it hidden under layers, both clothing and charm, but it never truly dulled. It watched the world with her. Felt things she hadn't yet learned to name.

Camilla stood beside her at the precinct desk, flipping through the latest reports with the same grim look she wore every time they had to blend back into the human world.

"Remind me again," Camilla muttered under her breath, "why we're pretending any of this is just drug-related chaos and not, you know… apocalyptic vampire war?"

Isla gave her a sideways glance, whispering low. "Because the Commissioner doesn't believe in vampires, and if we tell the force the truth, they'll either think we've cracked or they'll try to fight something they don't understand. Either way? Bodies."

Camilla sighed and jabbed a pen against the margin of the report. "You know, I was a lot less stressed before

I knew shadow demons and ancient vampire kings were real."

Isla offered a thin smile, but her eyes lingered on the list of names in front of them, all murder victims. All drained, mauled, or torn apart. Feral attacks that made headlines as designer drug overdoses. Each incident had left more questions than answers… until now.

A pattern was forming.

She tapped her finger over the last three crime scenes. "These line up too perfectly," she murmured. "It's a ring. Not random. They're closing in on something."

Camilla's brow furrowed. "Or circling something."

Isla's lips pressed into a thin line. "A nest. Or worse, a tomb."

They packed up and left the precinct within the hour, their cover intact, alibis airtight. But tension hung in the air like a taut wire. Isla's phone buzzed as they reached the car. Elias.

Elias: *What's taking so long? Meet at the safehouse.*

The others were already waiting when they arrived. Elias sat cross-legged on the floor amid a sprawl of books, old maps, and runes drawn in charcoal across aged parchment. Ronan leaned against the far wall, arms folded, the weight of leadership settling heavier across his broad shoulders by the hour.

"It's not just about power," Elias began without preamble. "Vaelric called it balance for a reason. The Crown was meant to tip the scales only when the world was already on fire."

Camilla raised a brow. "Cool. Guess we're mid-bonfire then."

Isla stepped forward. "What are you saying, Elias?"

He looked up. "You're not just marked by the Crown, Isla. You're *connected* to it. To the Old Ones, the original wielders. That mark burned into you because you survived the Veil. Because you refused the Hollow One's call. That's a bond none of the rest of us could ever survive."

Ronan straightened. "And that means she's the only one who can wield it. Use it."

"But if she uses it wrong," Elias warned, "if the balance doesn't reset after this… it could tear through her like wildfire. Like it did to the last bearer."

Silence dropped like a stone between them.

Isla swallowed hard. "Then we make sure it doesn't come to that."

She stepped forward, flipping the precinct murder board back onto the table. Red string criss-crossed the grid of crime scene photos and hand-sketched sigils. She stabbed a finger at the centre.

"Castlefield. The nest tunnels lead somewhere deeper. And the last three killings happened in a perfect crescent around it. Katerina's circling it for a reason. She's not just feeding or spreading chaos, she's creating a perimeter."

"A ritual site?" Camilla asked.

Ronan grunted. "Or a tomb."

Elias pointed to a second symbol on the map, the mark they'd found etched beneath the Peak District ruins. "This matches something I found in a Fae compendium from the early wars. A seal, used to bind something that couldn't be killed."

"Katerina's not trying to summon something new," Isla said slowly. "She's trying to *wake something up*."

The room fell into still silence.

Ronan exhaled through his nose. "Then we end it before it wakes. We strike first."

"How?" Camilla asked. "The vampire court's already turned us down once."

Isla met each of their eyes. "Then we don't ask for permission. We show them what's coming."

She turned to Elias. "What can I do with the Crown now? What can it *really* do?"

He hesitated. "Depends on how far you're willing to go."

She nodded once, eyes hardening like silver beneath a storm. "Far enough."

Ronan stepped forward, placing a hand briefly on her shoulder. "Then we go to war."

The safehouse was heavy with tension. A storm of supernatural chaos brewed outside, but inside, the team pored over maps, old texts, scattered reports, and hastily written notes. The walls were covered in red string and pinned photographs, faces of the missing, crime scene images, CCTV stills of ferals mid-rampage, and possible vampire sightings. Castlefield sat at the centre of it all. The eye of the storm.

Elias stood at the table, tracing Vaelric's words over and over on the parchment he had transcribed. "He said she was trying to rebuild the empire. Not just raise an ancient. But *rule* like them. Before the collapse. Before the Veil fractured and the balance was brokered."

"That would mean breaking every law the vampires have lived by since the old war," Isla said, arms crossed as she leaned against the edge of the table, her eyes flickering with a barely restrained energy. Since the Crown had burned into her skin, she felt... *more*. Stronger. Sharper. But also like something inside her had been pulled taut, humming like a blade waiting to be drawn.

"Blood magic," Elias muttered. "And if Vaelric is right... she's feeding that magic to the resting place of this ancient vampire she's trying to raise."

"She's risking everything," Ronan growled, pacing by the fireplace. "Not just her people. If the balance falls, the humans will find out. There will be no hiding what we are anymore."

"And they'll come for us all," Isla added quietly.

Camilla looked up at her. "Then we stop her before she gets the chance. But how do we even get to her? That nest is crawling with ferals."

Elias looked to Isla. "You said the mark responds to magic. What if it can be used to get through the Circle?"

Isla hesitated. "You want me to walk into a feral horde and hope this mark lets me through?"

"I think you were *chosen* to carry it," Elias said. "That crown, it's a symbol of peace. Of unity. Katerina's using fear to build her empire. But you, you're something different. You don't stand for one side."

"I left the pack. I don't follow the vampire courts. You're right, I don't belong to either," Isla said, the fire in her voice rising. "Maybe that's why it chose me. I'm not part of the old war."

"So... what do we do about backup?" Camilla asked. "The police won't exactly help us storm a vampire hideout."

"We *could* go to the wolf council," Ronan offered reluctantly. "Let them know what's coming. But they might see it as our fight, not theirs. And if they say no…"

"Then we go to your pack," Isla said, glancing at him.

Ronan looked at her for a long moment, then nodded. "They'd follow me. Enough to get us through the outer rings. But they'll need to know what we're walking into. I can't put them in this kind of danger unwillingly"

"We tell them the truth," Isla replied. "That a vampire wants to break the covenant and plunge the world into chaos. That she's using humans as weapons. That if we don't stop her now, there might not be a next time."

"But we ask. Because we need every sword, every claw, every ounce of strength we can gather."

Silence fell as they each absorbed the weight of what was to come. The plan was still forming, pieces moving into place, but the path was clearer now. The final strike would have to be precise, fast, and devastating.

Isla lifted her shirt slightly, exposing the faint glow of the mark burned into her skin, its lines subtle but pulsing, alive. "This... whatever it is. It's our way in. And maybe it's our only chance to stop her."

Camilla raised an eyebrow and smirked. "So... any chance it gives you shadow powers again? Or, I dunno, fire breath? Mind Control?"

"Let's hope it just keeps me alive," Isla muttered.

But inside, she felt it, the quiet hum of something ancient now nestled beneath her skin. The Crown hadn't just marked her. It had *claimed* her.

And whatever came next... she was ready.

Chapter 34: Blood in the Moonlight

The air outside the stone-walled council chamber was cold, sharp like a blade. Isla's boots echoed off the flagstones as the team stepped into the shadowed courtyard of the Wolf Council's ancestral seat, hidden in plain sight in the moorlands above the city, nestled in ancient stone ruins that humans chalked up to history and erosion. Ronan walked beside her, his jaw tight, the furrow between his brows deep with worry and purpose.

Inside, the council had listened. Grudgingly. Warily. And with the weight of centuries behind their eyes.

"You've brought proof," one of the Alphas had said, eyes flicking to the faint glow of the Crown's mark on Isla's chest, even hidden beneath her shirt. "But the path you ask us to take? It risks all."

The Council spoke of the Blood Moon, the ancient awakening rites, something even most wolves thought was lore and fearmongering. But the council had known what was happening. They'd watched. Waited. They would act, but only when the time demanded it.

If what they said was true, time was fleeting and the dead would rise on the next Blood Moon if Katerina wasn't stopped.

"Three nights," said Elder Niamh, her voice dry as wind-blown ash. "You must stop her. If Katerina's ritual begins, we will answer the call. Until then... gather your allies. Prepare."

The council hall was eerily still when Isla stepped away from the circle of Alphas. Their eyes tracked her like wolves scenting a storm, curious, wary, uncertain of the lightning that brewed in her chest.

Ronan walked beside her in silence, his jaw tight. Behind them, Camilla and Elias followed, the latter flipping through a charred old grimoire Vaelric had handed over, muttering incantations and interpretations under his breath. Camilla, ever grounded, kept her hand on the hilt of her weapon, eyes scanning the tree line as they descended the long stone steps away from the hidden council enclave.

"Well, that could've gone worse," she muttered. "Could've gone better, too."

"They knew," Isla said, voice low and sharp. "They've been watching. Letting us bleed while they sat on their thrones."

"They weren't going to move unless they saw the storm coming for them." Ronan cast a glance back at the council's great hall, its carved stone facade now swallowed again by forest shadow. "Now they know, Now they'll be ready."

"They said they'd call the packs only if necessary," Isla said. "What if they decide it isn't?"

"Then we show them it is."

But the conversation ended there.

A low growl echoed from the underbrush.

Isla's hackles rose instantly. The sharp scent of blood hit her nose before the shadows moved, ferals, a dozen at least, spilling from the trees like rats from a sewer. Their eyes gleamed, hollow and ravenous. Their mouths dripped crimson. One still wore the uniform of a city construction worker, his high-vis vest stained with gore.

"Ambush!" Elias shouted, already backing up, hands glowing as he summoned the wards Vaelric had taught him.

"Down!" Ronan shouted, already shifting. Bones snapped, his body elongating, fur bursting from skin in a heartbeat. A snarl erupted from his throat as he launched toward the first wave.

Camilla drew her gun, already firing. "I thought this was supposed to be a sacred place!"

"They don't care!" Elias barked, a shimmer of power curling around his fingers, glyphs lighting up along the lines of his forearms as he readied a spell. "They're beyond reasoning!"

Isla stood frozen for half a second, then the fire flared. Not around them. *In* her.

The mark on her chest blazed with heat. She doubled over, teeth clenched, breath coming in gasps. It was like a sun had ignited beneath her skin.

"Isla!" Camilla's voice cut through the chaos, laced with panic. "Get up! Get up!"

Her breath caught, heat licking along her spine, her chest alight with searing purpose. The Crown burned, the mark glowing molten gold through her shirt. Her fingertips crackled. Sparks. Heat. Flame.

Her heartbeat thundered, and the fire answered.

The energy exploded outward from Isla like a shockwave. Fire danced up her arms, but it wasn't burning her, it was part of her. Living flame in gold and crimson, licking at her fingertips like obedient snakes. Her eyes flared white, and when she looked at the ferals, they stopped. Just for a moment. Just long enough to see death staring back at them.

With a scream torn from her throat, she raised her hands, and from the ground, a shockwave erupted. Brimstone and heat cracked the earth beneath the ferals, sending several flying. One burst into ash mid-air. Another screamed as fire engulfed it, unholy howls shattering the trees.

Camilla ducked, wide-eyed. "Tell me that's you and not some fire demon joining the party!"

Isla didn't answer. She couldn't. Something ancient had awakened, something old and threaded with the very magic that bound their world together.

Ronan snarled beside her, bloody and wild but still grinning as he tore down another feral. "Looks like the Crown finally opened the damn door."

"I didn't open anything," Isla growled, eyes glowing amber-gold. "It opened *me*."

The fire responded like a creature unchained. With every swing of her fists, it burst outward, blasting through the attackers with blistering force. One shrieked as it turned to ash before their eyes. Another lunged and was caught mid-air by a chain of flame that wrapped around its limbs and yanked it down, into the dirt, searing flesh and bone.

Ronan, half-covered in blood, paused mid-slash to stare.

"What the hell?" Camilla breathed, wide-eyed.

"I don't know," Isla said, her voice raw and thunderous. "But I think it just woke up."

As the fire in her veins roared. The ferals hesitated now, their instincts faltering, sensing something they couldn't place, something beyond even vampire bloodlust.

Elias threw a spell that knocked three ferals back into the treeline. "We need to go! They'll keep coming!"

Ronan shifted back mid-run, breath heaving, body bloodied but alive. "We hold long enough to make them think we're retreating. The council are safe in their chambers. Then we finish this and get back to the city."

Camilla reloaded. "So, good news: you're a badass flame goddess now. Bad news: we've just pissed off every feral in the north."

The last feral broke and ran, shrieking into the trees.

The forest fell silent again. Elias stepped forward, brushing ash from his coat, his expression unreadable.

"That wasn't normal magic," he said softly. "That wasn't anything I've seen."

"The crown," Isla whispered. Her hand went to her chest where the brand still glowed faintly. "It's not just a mark. It's something more. Power... connected to something old."

"You think you can control it?" Camilla asked, eyes narrowing.

Isla looked at the blackened circle of trees around them, the scorched earth, the bodies still smoking.

"I think I have to."

Ronan, wiping blood from his face. "You just turned the tide of a battle alone. If the council wasn't convinced before, they sure as hell will be now."

Elias looked down at the ground where one of the ferals had been disintegrated. His fingers brushed the dirt, then stiffened. "They're getting bolder. Katerina's letting them off the leash."

"She knows we're close," Isla said. "We've got three days until the blood moon."

Camilla's gaze was like steel. "Then we take the fight to her."

They stood together, wind howling through the dark trees. Blood in the soil. Fire in the air. And the rising storm of war hanging on the edge of the moon.

The final battle was coming.

And this time, the monsters weren't hiding in the dark, they were coming for the city. Three nights until the Blood Moon. Three nights to stop the awakening.

And for the first time, Isla *felt* it. Not just fear. Not just strength. But a destiny touched by flame and shadow stood between them and the fall.

Chapter 35: Fire Before the Storm

The forest behind them crackled with embers and scorched earth, the stench of charred feral flesh thick in the air as Isla stood amidst the wreckage. Her breath came in short bursts, golden-red flames still flickering along the veins of her arms, her chest marked with the searing sigil of the Crown, a burning brand that pulsed with ancient power. She hadn't meant to let it out. But the ferals hadn't given her a choice. She was glad it had turned up, that she knew now what she was capable of.

Camilla stood to her left, panting, bloodied but alive, her jacket slashed but her grip firm on her weapon. Ronan growled low, scanning the shadows for any lingering threats. Elias, cloak torn and shirt singed, stared at Isla in awe and fear, something had shifted. Something vast. Something old.

No one spoke as they made their way back to the road. The sky was beginning to pale with dawn, and with it came the cold reality that they were running out of time.

Three days.

Three days until the Blood Moon.

Three days until Katerina tried to awaken the ancient vampire lost to time and myth, Valik, the Butcher-King of the old world. And every passing hour gave her more strength, more followers, more chaos to feed the blood magic she needed.

As they drove through the outskirts of Manchester, the city skyline a fractured mirror of lights and storm clouds, Ronan reached out to his pack. In whispers carried by the tether of Alpha to kin, he called for those still loyal to the balance to meet them at the old mill just south of the city centre.

But that wouldn't be enough. Not this time.

Elias scrolled furiously through an ancient tome, muttering under his breath about the sigil Isla now bore. "The Crown of Ash wasn't meant to be worn," he said, finally breaking the silence. "It was meant to be wielded by one chosen, one forged in both realms, touched by fire and shadow. That's you now."

"Doesn't feel like a blessing," Isla muttered, her fingers still tingling with the afterburn of power.

"You summoned flame from the earth, Isla," Elias replied. "And the ferals ran from you. That mark terrifies them. It's not just magic, it's law. Old, old law. Like vampire bloodline oaths, like fae pacts.

You've become something more than a wolf, more than a detective. You've become a symbol."

Camilla smirked faintly. "You always gotta outdo the rest of us, huh?"

Isla gave a dry laugh. "Didn't ask for this."

"Well, next time try not to light a forest on fire while not asking," Camilla shot back.

As the car slowed near a turnoff, a lone figure stepped into the road, tall, cloaked in twilight and armed with a silver-edged blade Isla recognized in an instant.

Selene.

The exiled Shadowblade. The enforcer of Seabright. The enemy turned Allie?

"You're late," Selene said, voice sharp and cool, but her smirk betrayed a familiarity. "Didn't think I'd miss the end of the world, did you?"

Camilla raised an eyebrow. "Is there, like, a secret WhatsApp for supernatural badasses, or…?"

Selene glanced at Elias. "He sent a raven. Very traditional."

Elias coughed, a bit sheepish.

Selene stepped closer, studying Isla with quiet calculation. "You wear the Crown. That changes things."

"We need help," Isla said simply. "And we need it fast."

Selene nodded. "You'll have it. I've rallied remnants of the Hollow Guard. And Seabright won't stay neutral for long once they realize what Katerina's truly trying to awaken." "Look, we may not be friends but with a common enemy we can be allies"

A low growl sounded from behind the buildings as Ronan's pack arrived, half-shifted, snarling, ready. They were joined by two others, wolves from rival packs under the same Alpha treaty.

The balance was beginning to tilt.

But as the first warning sirens screamed from the city's edge, they realized they were already too late for peace.

More ferals were loose, packs turned into mindless predators by Katerina's blood rites. They came clawing through the city centre, slaughtering anyone in their path, drawn toward Castlefield like moths to flame. Toward the final ritual site.

And they had three days to stop it.

Isla gritted her teeth, turning toward the smoke beginning to rise above the rooftops.

"Then we make a stand," she said. "We fight. We burn through them if we have to."

Selene drew her blade, firelight dancing along its edge. "Let them come."

And with allies gathering, flames rising, and the veil between realms growing thinner by the hour, they descended into the city once more.

To meet war with fire.

To meet fate with fang.

Chapter 36: The Gathering Storm

The skies over Manchester darkened far earlier than they should have. The city buzzed with its usual chaos, oblivious to the war quietly spilling through its cracks. But those attuned to the old blood could feel it, the hum of ancient power stirring, vibrating through the veins of the supernatural. The countdown had begun.

Back at the safehouse, tension had settled over the group like smoke. Plans were scattered across the table, maps of underground tunnels, patrol routes, aerial images of Castlefield and the surrounding ruins. Isla stood at the head, Ronan at her side, Selene just behind them, arms crossed and gaze sharp. Camilla leaned forward on the table, eyes narrowed, while Elias scrawled notes furiously into one of his bound journals.

"We have no time we have to move tonight," Isla said, her voice low. "Get through the perimeter. Get inside and disrupt whatever Katerina is planning before the ritual begins."

"They've been swarming in," Ronan added. "More ferals than I've ever seen, no control, no order. Just rage."

Selene stepped forward, golden eyes gleaming in the dim light. "She's creating chaos to keep us off balance. But there's a rhythm to it, her moves aren't random. She's stalling us."

"And letting fear do the rest," Elias muttered. "I've seen this kind of strategy before in texts from the last war. Divide, distract, and drain the enemy. She's playing her pieces while the real game happens elsewhere."

"Which is why we go in tonight," Isla said. "Before she's ready. Before the moon turns red."

They'd sent word to the smaller packs Ronan trusted. And the Wolf Council, reluctantly, had pledged aid. Warriors from the moors, forests, and hills surrounding the city were on the move, gathering quietly, waiting for the signal.

"Castlefield is our entry point," Isla continued. "There's a tunnel system beneath it, Elias thinks it feeds directly to the main chamber. Katerina will be there. That's where we strike."

"But first," Camilla cut in, "we survive tonight."

Because as she spoke, the night air outside thickened, filled with the low growls and scraping claws of the ferals that had found them.

Manchester Streets

The city screamed.

Shadows leapt from alleyways. Creatures barely human lunged through storefront windows, shrieking with bloodlust. Civilians scattered, police overwhelmed, and in the centre of it all, Isla's team surged forward.

Isla tore through a feral with claws now half-forged in flame. The fire that burned in her chest, the mark of the crown, was beginning to manifest in ways none of them could yet understand. She burned cold, focused, precise.

Camilla fired into the onslaught with grim determination, covering Selene's flank as the half-witch danced through the battlefield with lethal elegance. Ronan, a blur of muscle and fury, was fighting with the unyielding resolve of a pack alpha with everything to lose.

And Elias.

Elias muttered a word under his breath, a spell old enough to rattle the teeth in your skull, and a shield of spectral light flared outwards, hurling three ferals back into a wall with a crunch.

"We can't hold this line much longer!" Selene shouted, blood dripping from claw marks on her arm.

"We don't have to!" Isla roared back. She extended a hand, and the street beneath the ferals cracked, flame blooming in a spiral. Her powers, still wild, still learning her, answered the threat with fury.

As the last creature fell, the team stood heaving, soaked in blood and smoke.

"We lost ground on the western edge," a wolf scout growled, limping towards them. "They're everywhere."

"We need to strike *tonight*," Isla said again, voice firm. "We regroup. We hit Castlefield. Katerina doesn't get her blood moon."

The others nodded, exhaustion hidden beneath resolve. They would move as one, wolves, witches, hunters, and those who no longer fit cleanly into any category at all.

And in the darkening skies above Manchester, the moon was beginning to shift, tinged ever so faintly in red. Time was of the essence, the blood moon was closing in.

March to Castlefield

The city pulsed with an eerie stillness, the kind that settled in just before a storm broke the sky open. Isla stood atop the derelict rooftop of an old mill in Ancoats, its windows shattered, its brickwork bleeding history. The wind stirred her dark curls, and beneath her skin, the Crown's brand thrummed like a second heartbeat, hot, steady, alive.

She could feel the shift in the air. Something was coming.

Behind her, Camilla checked weapons, muttering quietly to herself, half ritual, half distraction, while Elias finished drawing a fresh warding circle in chalk across the floor, lacing it with threads of old Fae magic. Selene stood beside Ronan, speaking in low tones. Though it had been years since Isla had seen her, the witch looked unchanged, regal, lethal, eyes like carved amethyst.

"We don't have time for hesitation," Isla said. "Katerina's nest is fortified, ferals are swarming every exit into Castlefield, and if she completes the rite on the night of the blood moon"

"She won't," Ronan cut in. "Not if we hit her now and fast. The packs are waiting for my signal."

Isla nodded, turning to the map Elias had pinned across a broken slab of concrete. "There are three points of access," she pointed. "North, through Deansgate Locks. South, under the city via the disused Metrolink tunnels. And the west wall, the river path, it's narrow, risky, but could be a way in unnoticed."

"The ferals are nesting through the tunnels," Elias added. "I did a sweep earlier. They're guarding something… or someone."

Selene's gaze flicked to Isla. "She's bolstered by more than just bloodlust. She's been promised power, and ancient magic is coiling under that district. I can feel it."

Isla met her eyes. "Then we cut through the city and split forces. Selene, take the left flank through the river path. Ronan, bring your pack in from the north. Camilla and I will take the tunnels with Elias."

"Split up?" Camilla raised a brow. "That's bold."

"It's war," Isla said. "She's drawing power from fear and chaos. If we hit all fronts, she won't have time to rally them."

Elias added, "I'll lay traps through the tunnels. We'll draw them into a choke point."

Camilla loaded her weapon. "And I'll bring the bang."

A howl split the dusk air, low and resonant.

Ronan smiled. "They're here."

From the alleys beyond the mill, shapes began to emerge, wolves in human skin, powerful, silent. The Alpha packs of the North, South, and East, come to answer the council's call at last. Selene raised her hands and sent a pulse of violet light spiralling into the sky. It flared, then fractured like a signal fire.

Isla's blood surged. The brand on her chest flared once, searing her nerve endings. She inhaled sharply, flames flickering beneath her skin.

"The Crown is responding," Elias whispered. "You're waking, Isla."

Camilla gave her a sideways glance. "Shadow powers again? Or are you just going to start setting things on fire now?"

"Let's find out," Isla smirked.

They began the march toward Castlefield as the sky darkened and the city's heartbeat grew faint beneath the weight of what was to come.

Three fronts. One objective. Stop Katerina.

But Isla couldn't shake the chill crawling across her spine.

Something, someone, was watching. And it wasn't Katerina.

The moon hung heavy above Manchester, cloaked in clouds that churned like restless spirits. Every light in the city felt dimmer, as if the coming blood moon had already begun to cast its shadow. The streets buzzed not with traffic or nightlife, but with fear, an unspoken current rippling through the city's veins.

Inside the old, converted warehouse that now served as their war room, Isla stood over a worn map of Castlefield, the ancient tunnels beneath it marked in thick red ink. Around her stood Ronan, Camilla, Elias, Selene, and a handful of Ronan's packmates, all hardened warriors in their own right.

"We strike at nightfall," Isla said, voice firm. "Three nights until the blood moon. If Katerina completes whatever ritual she's planning, we won't survive the aftermath."

Selene nodded, brushing a stray white braid over her shoulder. "This isn't just about your city anymore. The balance is tipping too far. If Katerina awakens an ancient like the one she's trying to bring back..." Her lips thinned. "It'll be a massacre."

"She's raising the dead to build a throne," Ronan growled. "We tear it down before she ever sits on it."

Elias tapped a symbol on the map. "This, here. The old Roman bathhouse. The tunnels under it are closest to the den's entrance. It'll be heavily guarded."

"Then that's where we hit first," Isla said. "Selene, can you take the flank with three of Ronan's wolves? Camilla and I will breach from the north. Ronan, front line. You lead the charge through the fire."

Camilla gave a low whistle. "You're getting good at this whole 'commanding doom missions' thing."

Isla smirked. "Don't get used to it."

As the group began to split and prepare, Isla paused beside Elias. "Any progress on the glyphs Vaelric showed us?"

"Some," Elias said. "The mark of the Crown seems to amplify elemental energy, but not just any. Your power is tied to purification, Isla. Fire, yes, but it's more than that. It can burn away corruption, even in the blood."

"Useful," she said. "Especially if Katerina's blood-magic army is held together by whatever foul ritual she's cooked up."

"We still don't know who she's trying to awaken," Elias muttered. "But if Vaelric's theory is right, it's a vampire old enough to predate even the courts."

"Then we don't let her finish."

First Wave

They moved like shadows through the tunnels, packs split and coordinated across the city, converging on the heart of the rot. The air grew colder the closer they came, the stale breath of death and decay thicker in their lungs.

The first ferals came at them near the canal junction, emaciated bodies lunging from sewer grates and crumbling walls. But these weren't aimless like the others had been. They moved with something else behind their eyes now. Purpose. Direction.

Isla's claws extended mid-leap, slashing through the first feral as fire exploded from her skin, coating her arms in glowing flame. She didn't flinch. Instead, she embraced the power coursing through her like it had always belonged to her.

A burst of ferals surged toward Camilla, but Selene intercepted, twin daggers spinning like silver lightning.

She moved with an elegance beyond the supernatural, her form a blur of fury.

"Where do they keep coming from?" Camilla shouted, ducking under a swing.

"Rats multiply in the dark," Elias muttered, casting a pulse of arcane light that blinded three of the creatures. "But these ones have a master."

They fought through the wave, ground slick with ash and blood. One of Ronan's packmates fell, dragged down by three snarling ferals. Ronan's howl split the night, his fury igniting his shift mid-charge. The beast he became tore through them like paper.

More ferals emerged, pouring from crumbled archways and broken vents. Isla raised her hand and fire danced in her veins again. She brought her palm to the tunnel's ceiling and willed the fire forward. A burst of radiant flame erupted in a circle around them, halting the surge for mere moments, but enough.

"Move!" she screamed. "Push through!"

The streets were no longer quiet. They breathed war.

Manchester, in its tangled history of old and new, had never seen anything like this. From Spinningfields to the broken brick edges of Castlefield, the supernatural underworld had erupted into brutal chaos. The team had mobilised everything they had, every ally called, every loose end burned away in fire and blood.

And now, as the first wave of battle struck, it did so with the fury of centuries held in silence.

The team moved as one, flanked by members of Ronan's pack and a handful of fae warriors who had pledged allegiance after Lirien's intervention. Selene had returned, battle-worn and elegant as ever, blades hidden in the folds of her coat, her presence like ice slashing through the burning tension.

"They're already here," Isla said, voice low, eyes fixed ahead. Her nostrils flared.

"Let them come," Ronan growled beside her, eyes glowing gold in the dim light.

Camilla checked her sidearm. "Let me guess, bullets won't help?"

Elias shook his head. "Not unless they're blessed, silvered, or dipped in ash from a cursed pyre. So… probably not."

Camilla rolled her eyes. "Wonderful."

Ahead, the ruins of Castlefield opened like the throat of some ancient beast. The entrance to the underground nest loomed, dark and cracked, pulsing with a cold wind that smelled like copper and death.

Then the ground shook.

The ferals didn't wait for introductions. They launched again from shadows, gaunt, twisted creatures that had once been human, now feral vampires driven mad by Katerina's failed transformations.

One of them slammed into the first line of werewolves. Claws ripped, teeth snapped. Ronan ran, tearing into the creature before it could kill.

To Isla's right, Selene ducked low, slicing through two at once with blinding speed. Blood sprayed like black ink.

Isla stood in the middle of it all, her body vibrating, the mark of the Crown burning like molten iron across her chest. Something inside her cracked open.

A feral launched at her.

She didn't dodge.

She reached up, and flames erupted from her palm, swallowing the creature in white-hot fire laced with the scent of brimstone. It screamed, writhing, burning from the inside out. The mark pulsed again.

Wave after wave came, not just ferals now, but Nightborn, Katerina's chosen. These were faster, stronger, created as they should with the vampire councils blessing, at their own choice. They came with blades of bone, and mouths that whispered things not meant for human ears.

Ronan took a blow to the side protecting Elias, snarling as he went down to one knee, only to surge back up and rip through a Nightborn's throat with his claws.

Selene faltered under the weight of two more, until Camilla threw a blessed knife straight into one's heart. "You okay?" she shouted.

Selene grinned, bloodied. "I'm enjoying myself more than I should."

Even Elias was fighting, warding spells humming in his hands, magic carved into the earth around them like circles of sanctuary.

They fought through Lower Byrom Street and back into Castlefield proper, taking one bloody street at a time. With every block, they pushed Katerina's forces back, but it wasn't easy. It wasn't clean.

Bodies lined the pavement. Blood stained the cobblestones.

By the time they breached the outer edge of the nest, the team was battered, breathless, and burning.

The Calm Before the Next Storm

Inside the ruined courtyard, they paused. Isla's mark was glowing like a live brand beneath her shirt. Her breath steamed in the air despite the heat of the battle.

Elias looked at her with awe and something like fear. "That mark… it's waking up. That kind of power wasn't meant for prolonged use. It's connected to the balance of things. If it breaks…"

"It won't," Isla said, jaw tight. "I won't let it."

"But what if it isn't up to you?"

A silence followed. Even Camilla didn't break it.

Ronan stepped forward. "Three nights. That's all we have. We've pushed through the first line. The real war waits inside."

From deep below the ruins, a rumble answered him. Like something ancient had heard… and stirred.

Selene raised her head, eyes glowing silver. "They know we're here."

And so did Katerina.

They had won the first wave.

But the Blood Moon was still to come.

And the final battle was only just beginning.

Chapter 37: The Courtyard of Ruin

Smoke coiled through the broken stone pillars of what had once been a quiet, forgotten courtyard in the shadow of Castlefield. Now, it was a battlefield waiting to erupt. The scent of old blood, ash, and something older, darker, hung thick in the air. Isla stood at the front, her breathing slow and steady. Around her, the ragtag alliance they'd pulled together bristled with tension: Ronan's wolves, hardened and snarling at the scent of vampire filth; Selene, her twin blades humming with ancient enchantments; and even two Fae emissaries, cloaked in glamour and menace, stood poised with unreadable expressions.

"They know we're here," Camilla muttered, checking the clip in her modified pistol. "Like, *really* know. Look at this place."

The ground beneath their feet had started to pulse faintly with an unnatural rhythm, like a heartbeat beneath the stone.

"They've been preparing for this," Elias said grimly, eyes flickering to a network of carved sigils spiderwebbed across the flagstones. "The castle's saturated in old magic. Vampire wards... blood-forged. They're expecting a siege."

"They're getting a war," Isla growled.

The first scream came from above, a high, feral shriek as a figure leapt from the broken roofline, eyes glowing crimson, fangs bared. The courtyard *exploded* into motion.

The fight began in brutal earnest.

A half-shifted wolf launched upward to intercept the diving vampire mid-air, their bodies slamming into a wall with bone-crunching force. More figures emerged from the ruined arches, ferals, gaunt and rabid, no longer thinking, just *hungering*. Their movements were erratic, vicious, terrifying. They came in waves, howling and hissing.

Isla called to the fire.

The mark of the Crown pulsed against her chest, and with a roar, flames burst from her outstretched hands, sweeping low like a living thing. The front line of ferals ignited in a horrifying cascade of fire, shrieking and writhing.

"I guess shadow powers are off the table," Camilla shouted over the roar, ducking under a feral's swipe and planting a silver-dipped dagger between its ribs. "You're full-on inferno girl now!"

Ronan's axe was a blur, cutting through two vampires in a single swing, blood spraying the air. "Focus!" he barked, dragging Isla back-to-back with him as more poured in from a crumbling side passage.

"They're trying to split us up!" Selene called from the other end of the courtyard, cutting down two enemies in a single, graceful arc. Her blades shimmered with otherworldly light, one charged with sunlight, the other dipped in moonstone. "We push forward together, *now!*"

The Fae stepped in then. One raised a hand and whispered something in a language that made Elias's spine lock straight. Vines erupted from the cracks in the courtyard stones, snatching up a feral mid-leap, crushing it with a sickening crack. The other swept forward, her staff humming with a low resonance that shattered a vampire's illusions mid-attack, leaving it exposed for one of the wolves to rip apart.

They were gaining ground, slowly. Every step forward was blood-soaked and brutal.

"They're buying time for her," Isla said, turning to Elias as they moved toward the inner gates. "Katerina's inside. She's not fleeing, she's *waiting*."

"She wants the blood moon," Elias replied. "We interrupt her ritual before it starts, or we'll never stop it."

Another wave crashed into them, this time led by a pair of vampire knights, still intelligent, armoured, and wielding swords of blackened silver. One charged Isla directly, its speed inhuman, forcing her back. Their blades clashed, the heat from her magic warping the air between them.

He smiled, cruel and calm. "You're not ready for what she's bringing."

"I'm not here for her permission," Isla snarled, fire coiling around her arm like a whip, slicing through the air and melting half his chest plate before she plunged her blade through his heart.

The knight crumbled to ash.

Selene dropped beside her. "The gate's ahead, we make our stand there."

Isla looked around. They were bruised, bloody, but still standing. Behind them, the Fae held the rear. The wolves guarded the flanks. Camilla was reloading again, smirking despite the cuts on her cheek.

"Ready?" Isla asked the group, her eyes glowing faintly gold beneath the firelight.

Ronan cracked his neck. "Always."

"Let's finish this," Selene added.

Together, they moved toward the iron gates of Castlefield, now twisted, broken, and flanked by shadows. The path was narrow, the odds worse than ever.

But they weren't turning back.

The Crown burned hot against Isla's chest. Something was coming. She could feel it in her bones.

And whatever it was, it would meet fire and fury head on.

Chapter 38: Blood and Ashes

The air was thick with the scent of burning ozone and wet stone, mist curling in serpentine tendrils around shattered brick and blackened steel. The ancient ruins of Castlefield loomed ahead, its once-forgotten foundations now the epicentre of chaos. Crumbling viaducts and narrow alleyways twisted like veins through the district, leading them deeper into the belly of the beast. The supernatural lay coiled in every shadow.

Isla stood at the front of the group, blood on her jawline, eyes sharp and glowing faintly with that new ember-hued light that had begun to pulse in her chest since she accepted the Crown of Ash. Around her, allies gathered, Selene, cold and focused with silver knives dancing between her fingers; Ronan's pack flanking either side, growling low as they shifted between human and wolf with brutal efficiency; and Elias at her back, his coat scorched but his grip steady on his staff as he readied another warding sigil. Even Camilla, smeared in blood and wielding a reclaimed blade, looked more fury than fear now.

Castlefield was a maze, and every corridor they moved through, every open square or echoing chamber, was a gauntlet. The first wave had been ferals, dozens, maybe more, all snarling with blood-matted hair and eyes like shattered glass. But now they faced something worse.

Fae.

Not the peaceful kind Ronan had parlayed with or those that fought at their side. No. These were the twisted remnants of the old pacts, darkened by blood magic and centuries of bitterness. They moved like liquid shadow, slipping through crumbled walls and descending from broken beams. Siding with Katerina in a bid to break the centuries old law's forged to bring peace. Greed. Desire. A longing for power not owed to them. One dropped directly in front of Isla, her curved blades flashing.

"You shouldn't have come," the fae hissed, eyes flickering with a violet sheen, its voice the sound of wind through dying leaves.

"I've come to end this," Isla answered, stepping forward.

The two clashed with an echoing crack, flame erupting from her palm as the Crown's power ignited in defence. Her blade caught the fae's left shoulder, searing the skin where steel met glamour. The creature shrieked, twisting, but Ronan was already on it. He crashed into the fae with his full weight in wolf form, pinning it and snapping its spine in a sickening crunch.

All around them, the battle raged. Camilla ducked beneath a blow, slashing upward and catching a feral clean across the throat. Selene leapt from a shattered ledge above, landing with both feet on another's back and driving her daggers through its ribs with deadly precision.

Elias stood at the heart of it, chanting under his breath as glowing runes exploded from his staff in pulses of force that scattered their enemies. His magic didn't kill, but it kept the fight level, buying precious seconds for others to land fatal strikes.

They were pushing forward now, inch by inch, clearing the last stronghold before Katerina's sanctum. The vampire woman hadn't shown herself yet. She was watching, waiting. Probably smiling in that cruel, knowing way of hers. But she knew they were coming, and the last of her guardians were bleeding.

Isla paused at the edge of a twisted archway that led down into Castlefield's submerged crypts. She could feel it, her heartbeat syncing with something deeper, older. The mark on her chest burned with heat and something like memory. A voice stirred in her mind, not words exactly, but a call to finish what had begun.

"We're almost there," Ronan said, stepping beside her and wiping blood from his blade. "But she's not going to run."

"No," Isla said, eyes narrowed. "She thinks she's already won."

From behind them, a howl rose, one of Ronan's pack, torn down by a fresh wave of ferals spilling in from the alleyways like roaches from the dark. Elias turned, hands already glowing again. Camilla was barking orders, rallying some of the remaining allies who had taken injuries but were still standing.

"We have to get through them," Camilla shouted. "Now, or we lose the momentum!"

Isla nodded once. "Then we finish this."

She stepped into the fray again, flame in one hand, steel in the other, and a fire in her heart that would not be quenched.

Behind her, Castlefield waited. And somewhere in its depths, Katerina prepared for the final battle.

The Long March

The night air was thick with smoke and ash, tinged with the copper sting of blood and the static buzz of magic. Castlefield loomed, its once-proud ruins now twisted into a fortress of shadow and stone. Whatever Katerina had done to it, the place pulsed with corrupted energy, a beacon of something dark clawing its way toward the surface. The blood moon was still two nights away, but already its light bled faint red into the sky, unnatural, wrong.

The courtyard behind them was a graveyard now, littered with the mangled remains of ferals, rogue fae, and corrupted beasts. But there had been losses on their side too, one of Ronan's pack had fallen, and two of the allied fae had vanished mid-fight, swallowed by something in the mist.

"I don't like this," Camilla muttered, reloading her weapon with trembling hands. "I thought this was supposed to be the first wave."

"This was the first wave," Elias said grimly, leaning heavily on his staff. Blood matted his side, but he hadn't complained once. "And we're not done yet."

Ahead, the ancient entrance to Castlefield yawned like a wound in the earth, overgrown and crumbling, except now something unnatural bled through the cracks. Thorned vines pulsed as if alive. Arcane wards shimmered briefly, twisting like oil across stone. And the air hummed with the unmistakable resonance of blood magic.

"We go in quiet," Isla said, voice low, eyes scanning every corner. Her hands still glowed faintly from the fight before, the mark of the Crown now pulsing softly at her collarbone like living fire beneath her skin. "If Katerina doesn't already know we're here, she will soon enough."

"She knows," Ronan growled, wolf eyes glowing golden in the gloom. "She's waiting."

A low howl broke the silence then, not Ronan's pack, but something else. It was followed by the rustle of movement through the ruins ahead, shadows sliding between fallen pillars and half-collapsed brickwork. The ferals were regrouping. A last stand, or the next line of defence.

Then a scream echoed, high and sharp, a wolf cry, followed by a blast of searing blue flame that lit the skyline for just a second.

"Selene," Elias said under his breath, smiling grimly. "She's already inside."

"Then we push," Isla snapped. "We get to her and keep going. We don't stop until we reach Katerina."

With a nod from Ronan, the pack surged forward. Isla took point, the mark of the Crown flaring bright, pushing through the growing dark like a blade of fire. Camilla flanked her, gun drawn, breathing steady. Behind them came Elias, weaving quiet wards to shield them from the worst of the ambient magic, and Ronan, a living weapon, claws bared, fury barely restrained.

The fight was chaos. Shadow-walkers, half-feral, half-faerie, leapt from the ruins, blades flashing, eyes wild. Magic rained from hidden archers perched in crumbling balconies, curses spiralling through the air. Ronan's pack hit them hard and fast, a coordinated blur of teeth and fury. The fae allies twisted between planes, striking from thin air, their weapons glowing with ancestral enchantments.

And Isla, Isla moved like fire. Every blow she landed sparked flame, every strike echoed with something deeper, older. The mark on her chest seared with every step forward, guiding her toward something unseen. She didn't know how she knew where to go, but she *did*. The Crown wanted her forward. Toward Katerina.

Selene met them at the base of the final stairs, bleeding, but standing, two feral bodies at her feet and her white hair wild in the wind.

"You're late," she growled, tossing Isla a blood-slicked blade.

"Had a few stops," Isla replied, gripping the sword in one hand and her own flaming dagger in the other.

"Then let's finish this," Selene said, turning to the towering black doors that led beneath Castlefield.

Above them, the moon pulsed darker. The blood moon was coming. And Katerina was nearly ready.

They had one shot left to stop her.

And Isla Crowley wasn't planning on missing.

Chapter 39: The Hollow Gates

Castlefield loomed before them, cracked cobbles bleeding red beneath the shroud of midnight clouds. The old canal basin was tainted with blood magic now, warped and twisted into something unrecognisable. Where once there had been echoing stone archways and peaceful waterways, there now stood blackened ruins pulsing with corrupted energy. The scent of rot, old earth, and burnt iron curled in Isla's nostrils like a brand.

"This was once a sanctuary," Elias muttered, voice tight with grief. "An old neutral ground during the last war."

"Now it's a killing field," Ronan growled, his claws halfway shifted as he scanned the shadows.

The group moved cautiously, Isla at the front, the mark of the crown etched like fire into her chest, hidden beneath the neckline of her jacket but burning with each step closer to Katerina. The fae and werewolf allies flanked them, the line thin but resolute. Selene was at Isla's side, blades drawn, her expression hard as ice.

Then came the scream.

It tore through the night like a knife through silk, inhuman, echoing through the gutted ruins.

"Positions!" Ronan barked. The pack dropped low, forming ranks.

A wave of ferals surged from the old tunnels that lined the basin, too fast, too wild, too hungry.

Their eyes glowed with corrupted crimson light, skin stretched tight over snarling faces, blood dried into cracked patterns across their chests. Some were barely recognisable as once-human. Others looked more like beasts, their limbs twisted, jaws broken wide like serpents.

They were monstrous… and unrelenting.

The first clash hit like thunder. Teeth met steel, claws tore through magic wards. Camilla fired point-blank into a feral's skull as it leapt at Elias, her bullets laced with powdered silver and spell-borne fire. Elias countered with a ward burst, sending another flying into the wall with a concussive boom.

"Keep together!" Isla shouted, driving a blade through a feral's chest, her eyes flashing with golden fury as the creature howled and disintegrated in a hiss of blood.

Selene moved like a storm, silent, deadly, efficient. She left a trail of severed limbs and broken bodies, the shadows curling around her in reverence. Her magic was ancient, steeped in balance and bound by her oath to preserve it.

And still they kept coming.

The second wave hit harder, larger ferals, more organised. One roared out commands in a language long dead. The old war tongue. They were being directed now.

"They're guarding her," Ronan spat, slamming into a beast twice his size and throwing it off a collapsed stairwell.

"She's close," Isla said, breathing heavy. The mark on her chest was glowing faintly, burning like fire behind her ribs. "She knows we're here."

"We have to push through." Camilla reloaded, her voice tight. "We don't get another shot."

"Then we burn the path open," Elias said, eyes flaring with resolve. He pulled a rune-laced grenade from his satchel and threw it forward. It exploded in a dome of searing blue flame, disintegrating three ferals and lighting the corridor ahead.

The ruined basin had become a labyrinth of broken stone and death. But Castlefield's heart lay ahead, through the archways shrouded in red fog, past the blood seals scrawled on the walls.

That was where Katerina waited.

They regrouped just outside the central chamber, their clothes torn, faces bloodied, magic nearly drained. But none of them faltered.

"We end this," Isla said.

"Or die trying," Selene agreed softly.

And then they stepped forward, the final veil ahead, a pulsing doorway of blood and bone that led into the heart of Katerina's domain.

Behind them, the air grew quiet. Before them, Castlefield's heart beat like a war drum.

The final battle had begun.

The Crimson Hall

The great stone door groaned on its hinges, shrieking in protest as Ronan shoved it open, his muscles straining. Beyond the threshold, a deep crimson glow poured from sconces high on the blackened stone walls, casting long, dancing shadows that crawled across the floor like living things. The team stepped through one by one, their footsteps swallowed by the vast, cavernous silence that greeted them.

The chamber was enormous, easily the size of a cathedral, its ceiling lost in darkness above. Massive arched columns lined the sides like skeletal guardians, ancient and cracked, wrapped in dried vines and faded runes. In the centre, a wide circular floor had been carved into the stone itself, a ritual circle inscribed with silver-inlaid glyphs that pulsed faintly with residual magic. The scent of old blood and scorched earth clung to the air, thick and cloying.

To the left, several passageways led off into deeper tunnels, each of them flickering with unnatural shadows. To the right, a raised platform overlooked the chamber, once perhaps a place of audience or judgment, now transformed into a throne of bone and black crystal. And there, seated like a queen awaiting her guests, was Katerina.

She sat lazily, one leg crossed over the other, her fingers draped elegantly along the armrest of her jagged throne. Her eyes gleamed like garnets in the low light, amused and electric with fury.

"You made it," Katerina said, her voice echoing like silk on stone. "Just in time for the end."

From the shadows, more of her turned ones stepped forward. Dozens. Feral vampires, eyes glowing with hunger, bodies twitching with madness. They lined the chamber walls, crouched on the rafters above, and emerged from the surrounding tunnels. They were everywhere.

Isla stepped forward first, her chest still glowing faintly with the mark of the crown. The heat within her pulsed like a second heartbeat, the fire under her skin waiting to be unleashed. Ronan flanked her on one side, Elias and Camilla on the other, the rest of their allies, Selene, a squad of Ronan's pack, and two fae warriors sent by Lirien, fanning out behind them.

"Then let's not disappoint," Isla said coldly.

The room exploded.

The ferals screamed in unison and surged forward like a tide of darkness. Ronan shifted mid-run, his massive wolf form colliding with a feral and slamming it into the ground with bone-crunching force. Selene danced through the chaos, twin daggers flashing, her movements impossibly fast and precise. The fae warriors unleashed arcs of green flame that cut through the charging horde, while Camilla emptied her sidearm with cold efficiency, every shot taking down another of the deranged creatures.

Isla moved like she was born to it. A feral lunged, and she met it with a roar, her body enveloped in a halo of golden fire. Her punch landed like a comet, hurling the creature back into a stone pillar that shattered on impact. Every movement she made was powered by the Crown's flame, controlled, directed, lethal.

But they were outnumbered. For every vampire that fell, two more seemed to rise.

Elias reached the ritual circle and began tracing runes in the blood-spattered stone, trying to disrupt the glyphs that pulsed with ancient energy. "This is part of the awakening!" he shouted over the roar. "She's been feeding the ritual with the blood from every victim!"

"Then stop it," Isla growled, throwing another vampire aside and shielding Elias with her body.

From her throne, Katerina watched, unmoving. Her eyes burned as she studied Isla, no longer amused, but calculating. She rose finally, her long coat falling open to reveal a corset of steel and leather, weapons strapped to her thighs. Her power radiated like a pulse, cold and suffocating, and the room seemed to darken around her.

"Do you feel it yet?" she said, her voice somehow cutting through the noise. "The pull of destiny? The truth behind the stories? You think this is about ruling Manchester?" She sneered. "This is about legacy. Evolution. Fire can destroy, yes… but it also cleanses."

Isla locked eyes with her, the flames at her fingertips igniting once more. "Then let's see which of us burns brighter."

Katerina smiled, and leapt into the fight.

The throne room became an inferno of battle.

Chapter 40: Shadow and Flame

The air cracked like thunder as the first vampire crashed into the earth in front of them, thrown from the ramparts above. Its eyes blazed crimson, face twisted with the hunger that marked it as one of Katerina's original brood, pureblood, ancient, and lethal. The room echoed with the roars and snarls of battle. Blood streaked the stone floor, and the clash of metal and fang was deafening.

Selene moved first, her long coat whipping behind her, hands wreathed in inky darkness. The ground beneath her feet writhed as shadows coalesced around her, answering her call. She spoke a word in an ancient tongue, and the shadows flared outward, snatching two ferals mid-leap and slamming them into the wall with a sound like wet pulp.

Isla felt it, Selene drawing on something more. The Crown's mark on her chest flared hot, reacting to Selene's magic. Selene turned toward her, eyes glowing faintly. "Take it," she muttered. "you've wielded more powerful shadows than this before."

Isla didn't question. The bond snapped into place like a lock clicking open. Isla felt the rush of power siphoning toward her, like black flame and silver steel. The shadows that danced around her grew darker, thicker, and more alive. With a flick of her wrist, she sent them spearing forward, staking a vampire through the chest before it could sink its fangs into one of Ronan's wolves.

"Shadowborn," one of the full vampires hissed. Its voice was gravel and ice. "You should've stayed in the Hollow."

Isla stepped forward then, drawing a long dagger etched in silver and iron. "You first."

Ronan was already in his shifted form, tearing through a line of ferals like a storm of teeth and fury. Blood drenched his coat, but he didn't stop. His wolves moved with precision, packs that had trained for this kind of battle for centuries, now loosed upon the city with the full blessing of the council.

But it wasn't enough.

From the darkened arches leading deeper into Castlefield's ruins, more of Katerina's vampires began to pour through. Not just ferals, but disciplined, elite fighters, older, smarter, and twice as deadly.

"Pull back!" Elias shouted, his voice sharp over the comms. "We need to regroup!"

Camilla, dual pistols in hand, dropped three with silver-loaded rounds before ducking behind the remnants of a stone pillar. "There's too many. We need air support, or a damn miracle."

And then the tide turned.

A vampire, taller than the rest, moved forward. Pale as moonlight, clad in a dark coat that shimmered with runes. One of Katerina's commanders, if not her mate.

He didn't fight with rage. He fought with control, every strike calculated, every move designed to kill. He cut through Ronan's second with a single motion and knocked Selene back with a burst of dark energy that turned the shadows on her to screaming wisps.

Isla's heart pounded.

They were losing.

She moved toward him, power boiling beneath her skin. The mark burned hot. The shadow stirred.

But the vampire merely smiled.

"You bear the Crown," he said, his voice like velvet over broken glass. "Do you even know what that means?"

Isla lunged, her blade meeting his in a shock of sparks. "I know enough to stop you."

They clashed, steel and fire, blood and shadow. Around her, her team was being pushed back. Even the wolves had started to falter.

Selene was on her knees, eyes blazing as she tried to summon the shadows again. Elias had drawn a ward into the earth, but it was cracking under the pressure. Camilla was out of bullets, her backup weapon drawn but her stance growing defensive.

"We need to fall back," Ronan growled. "Regroup, find another way in."

"No," Isla said through clenched teeth, dodging a swipe from the commander's claws. "If we do, we lose the chance."

A flare of shadow burst from her palm. The vampire shrieked as it caught him across the face, staggering him for the first time. Isla didn't hesitate, she drove her blade into his chest, forcing it through with all her strength.

He snarled, clawing at her, but the Crown's mark flared again, brighter now, burning through her shirt with searing white light.

And the vampire turned to ash.

For a moment, the courtyard stilled.

Then the others screamed in rage and descended like a wave of teeth and bone.

Isla turned to the others, blood streaked down her arm, power dancing across her skin.

"We hold the line," she said. "We push forward. Katerina is at the back we need to get to her to end this."

"And when we get to her?" Camilla called out.

"We end it," Isla answered, eyes burning. "Or we die trying."

Behind them, the wolves howled.

Ahead of them, Castlefield waited, ancient, cursed, and thick with shadow.

And somewhere within, Katerina was watching. Smiling.

The true battle had only just begun.

Blood and Ash

The Crimson Hall burned red with fury. Shattered marble columns loomed overhead like broken teeth, casting jagged shadows across the chaos. The air was thick with smoke, blood, and the metallic scent of magic. Screams echoed off the ancient stone, a harmony of rage, pain, and fury from both sides. The battle had long since become a blur of motion and instinct.

Isla stood at the heart of the storm, the mark of the Crown glowing fiercely on her chest beneath her torn shirt, a pulsing brand of fire and power. The body of Katerina's guardian lay at her feet, smouldering, his blood mingling with ash on the floor.

Ronan was at her side, fur matted with blood, his and others', fangs bared as he lunged at a feral that had broken through the line. Camilla had taken up a position against a pillar, reloading her weapon, lips tight in grim determination. Selene fought like a storm nearby, blades flashing silver against dark limbs, her movements dancing in deadly rhythm with Elias' magic, who stood at the eye of the maelstrom weaving shields and flame.

They had pushed farther than anyone expected. But Katerina wasn't done.

From the shadows beyond the broken dais, a tremor rolled through the ground. A ripple of heat. Of power. The very air shivered around them.

The next wave was coming. And ahead, somewhere cloaked in shadow and blood, Katerina waited.

They had made it to the heart of the nightmare. But getting in was only half the battle.

Chapter 41: The Final Strike

The air in the Crimson Hall crackled with magic, the raw, electrified energy of two forces clashing violently. Isla, Ronan, Elias, Camilla, and their unlikely allies, Selene, Ronan's pack, and the few surviving members of the Fae forces, fought in the shadows of Castlefield, their breath ragged, their bodies covered in blood. Every strike, every shout, was an echo of the storm brewing at the heart of this decaying fortress.

The walls of the hall, adorned with ancient symbols and sigils, seemed to breathe with life, twisting and shifting in response to the battle. The vampires were relentless, an endless tide of fangs, claws, and hunger. But now, with the power of the Crown, now a scar burned deeply into Isla's chest, she felt something shift. A heat rising within her that she barely understood, but it was starting to merge with her wolf instincts. The darkness of the veil she had crossed once before was at her fingertips, laced with fire and brimstone.

"Push forward!" Ronan's voice rang out through the chaos. His pack was a whirlwind of claws and teeth, carving through the ferals that continued to pour from the shadows. Their presence was overwhelming, and yet, the tide was beginning to turn in their favour, the pack slowly clearing a path to the heart of Katerina's domain.

Isla stood beside Ronan, her wolf-form shifting uneasily under the weight of her powers. The mark of the Crown burned with her, a strange heat that seemed to flicker and crackle around her every movement. As she reached down to land another brutal blow on the nearest vampire, she could feel the air distort around her, her powers, once reserved only for her wolf form, now extended to the very nature of fire, and the smell of sulphur hung heavy in the air.

"You're not ready for this!" Katerina's voice rang out above the fray, piercing through the chaos. Isla's senses honed in on the sound, and there, standing above them all, was Katerina, a vision of cold elegance amidst the destruction, her eyes glowing an unnatural shade of violet as she watched the fight unfold. Her minions continued to fight to the death, unwilling to allow the intruders any ground.

Katerina's laughter echoed through the Crimson Hall, a cold, malevolent sound. "You think you can stop me? I was born in the blood of war. This city, this world, it will bend to my will. You've already lost, Isla Crowley."

Isla's heart hammered in her chest. She didn't have time to analyse Katerina's words, she knew that the vampire queen was playing a different game, one where the rules were set to her advantage. Every time Isla got close, Katerina seemed to slither out of reach, keeping herself hidden behind layers of her army. But not this time. No more running.

"Not this time, Katerina," Isla growled, her voice laced with determination. She stepped forward, her chest tightening as the heat inside her grew, like a furnace fed by the dark energy of the veil itself. She lifted her hand, feeling the strange power swirling in her fingertips. Fire, brimstone, embers, and smoke, twisted and flared out from her palm.

The first wave of fire roared forward, searing through a cluster of Katerina's closest guards. The air exploded with heat, the vampires shrieking in agony as the flames engulfed them. For a moment, the world seemed to pause as Isla felt her powers surge with more intensity than ever before. She could taste the fire on the back of her tongue, feel it pulse through her blood.

"That's it, Isla," Elias shouted over the noise, his eyes wild with excitement and fear. "That's your power! It's the Crown! You can't stop now, finish this!"

Katerina's eyes locked onto Isla with an icy fury. The vampire queen raised her arms, an ethereal, shadowy aura coiling around her like a storm. "Fool," Katerina spat. "You cannot wield the power of the Crown. You will burn from within, like all who try to claim what they don't understand."

But as Katerina spoke, Isla felt the surge of strength inside her. She could feel it: Katerina's words were meant to break her, to cast doubt, to instil fear. Yet all they did was fuel the fire inside her.

The heat in her chest intensified until the mark of the Crown flared like a beacon, flames erupting from her as if the very soul of the crown had been summoned. The ground beneath them cracked and split with the power now coursing through Isla's veins. "Then let's see if I burn," she hissed.

Suddenly, Ronan's pack broke through the last of the vampires surrounding them, forcing their way into the centre of the Crimson Hall. Isla felt the shift, felt Katerina's grip on the battle falter as her guards were overwhelmed.

Katerina's expression twisted into one of rage. "You think you're worthy to challenge me?" she hissed, her eyes glowing brighter, deeper. "You think you can stop the awakening? You are nothing but a pawn!"

The tension in the room mounted, the stakes higher than ever.

But just as the battle seemed to reach its apex, a figure appeared in the doorway, a shadowy, silent form that none had anticipated. Standing tall, backlit by the dim torchlight of the hall, was a figure cloaked in darkness.

"You should have known this was never your fight, Katerina," Dorian's voice was as cold as ice, filled with a finality that sent chills down Isla's spine.

Katerina's eyes widened in disbelief, as if the very last shred of her plans unravelled in an instant. "You," she whispered.

Dorian gave a small, almost imperceptible smile. "Always."

Before Katerina could react, Dorian's hand shot forward, spearing Katerina straight through her heart

He stepped forward, his face calm, his eyes dark and unreadable. In one swift motion, he raised his hand, and the room grew silent, as if the very air had stopped moving.

For a long moment, there was nothing but silence, the smoke and ash from the battle hanging in the air like a shroud.

And then, with a swift motion, Dorian turned to Isla and the team. "It's over. For now," he said, his voice filled with quiet certainty.

Isla's heart pounded in her chest as she stared at the aftermath of the chaos. Her eyes met Dorian's, and for a split second, she saw something unreadable in his gaze.

Before anyone could react, he vanished into the shadows, leaving the team to process the final moments of the fight.

As Katerina's body lay still, Isla realized that the fight for control was far from over. But what had just happened, what Dorian had done, was a game-changer.

The stakes were higher than they had ever been, and this was only the beginning.

"What the hell just happened?" asked Camilla

Thank you for reading the first book of The Bloodbound Covenant series!

Your journey through the streets of Manchester, filled with secrets, supernatural intrigue, and fierce battles, has only just begun. Isla, Ronan, Camilla, Elias, and the rest of the team have faced their first major threat, but with Katerina's plans still unfolding and new, even darker forces on the horizon, the war for the supernatural world is far from over.

As we close this chapter, remember that the true danger has yet to reveal itself, and the stakes will rise even higher in the next book. The battle for the bloodline, peace, and survival will continue to evolve with new alliances, unexpected twists, and intense conflicts that will test everything our team has fought for.

Stay tuned for the next instalment of The Bloodbound Covenant series, where we'll dive deeper into the mysteries of the last war, the ancient laws of the supernatural world, and Isla's newfound powers. What will they uncover in their fight for survival? What sacrifices will be made in the quest to stop the true force threatening to destroy everything?

The adventure isn't over yet.

Epilogue

The dust of battle settled in the ruins of Castlefield, the weight of their victory barely sinking in. The air was thick with the scent of smoke, blood, and the lingering echoes of their fight. Katerina, the vampire who had threatened to unravel the fragile balance of power between the supernatural and human worlds, was dead, her life snuffed out in the most anticlimactic fashion imaginable.

Isla stood in the centre of the decimated courtyard, breathing heavily, her senses still on high alert. The lingering adrenaline rush from the fight pulsed through her veins, her heightened senses picking up the subtle changes in the air, shifts that told her the world wasn't quite as it seemed. The battle was won. The vampires were defeated. And yet, something gnawed at her gut, a warning she couldn't shake.

Ronan stood beside her, his chest heaving, face bruised from the feral onslaught. His pack members had done their part, clearing the way for their final confrontation. He'd fought like a beast, tearing through the enemy like the Alpha he was. But even now, his eyes kept darting toward the shadows, as if expecting something, someone, else to emerge.

"What now?" Camilla's voice was strained, but there was no relief in it. Not yet. She'd been right there with them, holding the line as Isla had brought her powers to bear. The human detective, now fully aware of the world that had collided with hers, was a part of this fight in ways she never could have imagined. Yet, she was still struggling to keep her footing, to understand what the hell was happening, even as the dust settled around them.

Elias, always the thinker, was already deep in his own mind. He stood apart from the group, his gaze distant, watching the ruins of Castlefield as if the answers to all their questions might appear from the wreckage. "This is just the beginning," he muttered, more to himself than anyone else.

But the real shock came not from the remnants of the battlefield, nor the looming questions of what came next, it came from the unexpected figure who had walked out of the shadows.

Dorian.

He had appeared out of nowhere, stepping from the darkness like some shadow that had always been there, waiting. Without a word, without hesitation, he had struck down Katerina with a swift, brutal motion. His face had been unreadable, his actions as swift and precise as ever. And then, just as quickly, he had vanished, melting into the night as if he had never been there at all.

The team had stood in stunned silence, watching his departure, none of them able to explain why he'd intervened, or why he hadn't been part of the battle to begin with. They had assumed Katerina was their fight, their responsibility to end. But Dorian's sudden arrival and swift execution had shattered that assumption. Now they were left with more questions than ever.

"What just happened?" Camilla's voice was a mixture of awe and confusion. She had fought beside Isla and seen things she never believed possible, but this? This was something else entirely.

"I don't know," Isla said quietly, her eyes scanning the ruins. There was a strange sense of finality in the air, yet also something unresolved, hanging just beyond her reach. "But I don't think it's over yet."

Dorian's intervention had been like a mark, an unsolved riddle on their victory. It wasn't just that he had killed Katerina, it was that he had done it without explanation, without any acknowledgment of who they were or why they had been involved in this conflict. For all his power, his skill, and his role in their world, he was still a mystery to them all.

Isla felt it in her bones: something bigger was coming. Dorian's actions had shifted the course of their battle, but they had only scratched the surface of a much deeper mystery, one that stretched far beyond the death of Katerina. She had always known this city, this world, was more complicated than it seemed. But now, she could feel it, the quiet hum of something ancient stirring beneath the surface. The crown, the powers awakening within her, the forces moving in the shadows, it was all connected.

"We need to figure out why he did it," Elias finally spoke, his voice a quiet resolve. "And what it means for the future."

"Let's not forget the bigger picture," Ronan added, his voice low. "Katerina may be dead, but whatever she was planning, whatever she's been involved in, isn't gone. There's more at play here. A lot more."

Isla nodded, her eyes narrowing as she took in the silent ruins of Castlefield. The battle had been won, but the war was far from over. Katerina may have been defeated, but the forces that had been set in motion were still out there, more powerful, more dangerous than they could have ever anticipated.

And somewhere, in the shadows of this world, Dorian was waiting. Watching. And Isla had no idea what role he would play in the battles yet to come.

But one thing was clear. The city of Manchester was far from safe. The lines between human and supernatural, between balance and chaos, were becoming harder to see. The blood moon was coming, and with it, the threat of something far more ancient and deadly than anything they had faced before.

As the wind shifted through the ruins, carrying with it the last remnants of their fight, Isla felt a chill settle deep into her bones. This was only the beginning. The game had changed. And they were no longer just hunting down vampires. They were about to become part of a war that had been brewing for centuries, one that would decide the fate of everything.

The questions that remained, about Dorian, about the truth behind Katerina's plans, about what lay beyond the veil, would wait. For now, the war was far from over.

Two more days until the Blood Moon!